MISSING *a* MASON GRAY *case*

by

WILLIAM C. MARKHAM

"presume nothing" - Sherlock Holmes

1

I liked the Deluxe Diner, though I'm not sure what was so deluxe about it. The service was shitty, but the coffee was good. Not that fancy cat-shit barista stuff they serve at Starbucks, but old-school coffee, the kind that comes with the little thumb-sized paper creamer containers that the waitress carries in her apron. Not that I ever take cream. I like mine black. Usually, I pocket the cream to take back to the office to feed to the stray tomcat that lives out back. One-eyed Willy. Yeah, I named him after the pirate from *The Goonies*. It's a good flick. But I digress.

I took another swallow. My coffee had gone cold. I waved at Lorraine for a refill, then struck a match and lit a Camel because I knew it would be a couple of minutes before she hobbled out from around the counter. I don't use a lighter. Sure, I carry one, just in case, but I rarely use it. The smoking experience is more visceral, more real somehow, when a match is used. I think it's that whiff of sulfur and the acrid fumes that burn the eyes a little. After taking a nice long drag, I set my cancer stick on the ashtray and watched the lacy ribbon of smoke climb its way toward the ceiling.

This was my booth. I never sat anywhere else—not that I had to, since the place was always empty. I'm not sure what I'd do if it got busy and my seat wasn't available. Sit somewhere else, I guess. But it was a good booth for me. The flickering neon sign just above the window created enough glare that someone outside had to look really hard to see in, but I could see out just fine. Not to mention my flat was right across the street.

Because the place was never busy, it was always quiet— and I like quiet. It makes for good thinking. And right now, I needed to think.

Outside, it was dark and raining. But this was no surprise. It had been raining for two weeks straight: not a constant deluge, but a light drizzle with intermittent showers interrupted by the occasional downpour. At least that's what the weatherman said. Right now, it was a downpour. Small rivulets of rainwater flowed down the window beside me, converging near the bottom before disappearing from view. The weather fit my mood perfectly.

I looked out to the ugly rose-colored building across the street and took another drag. My flat was on the second floor, and the light in the front window was still on. Of all the screwed-up things I've seen, this one beat 'em all. There was a dead man in my front room, and I had no idea how he got there.

***

I was working late at the office, which was pretty typical. I'm not much of a morning person, so I stay late to catch up on paperwork. It suits me fine; I get more work done when I'm there alone. My boss, Frank, is a good guy—actually, he's a great guy, one of the best—but he's a talker. About eight, I grabbed a couple of files I was working on, locked the place up, and went to meet a new client. Nothing special, just some accountant who suspected his wife of infidelity and needed evidence for the divorce proceedings. We get them all the time. It's a pretty simple job: follow the mark and snap a few compromising photos. We call it a "tail and nail."

After the meeting, I swung by the corner market to pick up some snacks and a bottle of gin. One of the perks of not having a car is that I can drink all I want and not worry about DWIs. Not that I'm an alcoholic; I just like my gin. It's like Christmas in a bottle. I headed on home after that.

As soon as the cab pulled up in front of my flat, I knew something was hinky. There was light coming from the front window. Most people would think they'd accidentally left the light on, but not me. I never, ever turn on the overheads. They hurt my eyes. I don't even know why I bothered putting bulbs in them when I moved in. If I have some reading to do, I turn on a

2

lamp. They all emit a nice, soft yellow glow, not the harsh white glare shining through the window.

I paid the cabbie and went around back. I always use the back steps; that way it's not so obvious when I come and go. At the top of the stairs I set the groceries down on my pathetic excuse for a balcony and drew my pistol from its shoulder holster, feeling the weight of its false reassurance settle in my hand.

I'd never shot anyone before, not even back when I was on the force. Sure, I went to the range on a regular basis, and I could put five out of six rounds in a three-inch bull's-eye at thirty yards, but there's a big difference between throwing lead at a paper target and at a living, breathing human being. It doesn't matter how good of a shot you are if you ain't got what it takes to pull the trigger when it counts. For a man with a soul, it takes conviction, a certainty that whoever's on the other end of that barrel deserves to die. Now, considering how the deadbolt was busted and the door was pried away from the jamb, I figured my first time might be right around the corner.

I nudged the door open with my foot and glanced inside, pistol leading the way. The kitchen, illuminated faintly by the living room light filtering down the hallway, was empty except for the pile of dishes in the sink. I stepped inside and eased the door shut behind me, muffling the noise of the outside traffic. I stood there quietly for a few minutes, listening for any movement in the place. Hearing nothing, I moved down the hallway, checking the bathroom on the right and the bedroom on the left, making sure they were both clear. At the end of the hall, I froze. Illuminated by the overhead light was a figure lying on the floor—a man in black jeans and a black T-shirt.

A dark puddle of blood emanated from his head and was slowly soaking into my area rug. Dammit, that rug had belonged to my grandmother; they'd better be able to clean it.

File folders and loose papers littered the floor around

him. My desk had been thoroughly ransacked.

I moved closer for a better look, being careful not to contaminate the scene. I could see two entrance wounds in the back of his head—small caliber—what the cops call a double tap. It was the sign of a professional hitter.

Certain now that the apartment was empty save for the corpse adorning my living room floor, I went back to the kitchen and grabbed a pair of gloves from "the drawer." I got the term from my mother. Anything that didn't have an otherwise logical home was tossed into it. With the gloves on, I carefully fished out the man's wallet.

By this point, my nerves were a little frazzled, so I went across the street to the diner to figure out my next move.

***

"Miserable night, ain't it, honey?" said a voice to my right, hoarse and gravelly, like a moped with a bad muffler. Lorraine had come by at last with the coffee. She once told me she'd been working at this diner for twenty-five years. *Twenty-five years.* Can you imagine? Coming to the same greasy hole in the wall, waiting on the same cheap bastards for eight hours every day with no chance of ever getting a raise. When I asked her why she stuck around, she said, "Well, honey, I been here so long I don't reckon I know how to do nothin' else." Damn. I'd have put a gun barrel in my mouth years ago.

"That it is, Lorraine," I replied without taking my eyes off the window.

"You all right? You look pale as a ghost."

"I'm fine," I lied. "Been a long day, is all."

"Well, if you need anything, you let me know," she said over her shoulder as she walked back to the counter.

Pale as a ghost. I didn't doubt it. At least my hands weren't shaking anymore. They hadn't started until I got to the diner. Guess it took a bit for the fear to settle in. I couldn't even drink my first cup of coffee without spilling it down the front of my shirt. Ten minutes and two smokes later, they'd finally quit. Now I just needed to slow my thought process and focus on one question at a time.

I took another long drag, savoring the harsh smoke that carried the precious nicotine into my blood. I remembered reading once that nicotine binds to the same receptors in the brain as adrenaline and promptly pictured two school boys fighting over who was going to sit in *that* seat. I hoped the nicotine was winning.

Glancing down at the dead man's wallet lying open on the table, I tried to place the face in the picture. I knew that face from somewhere, but it was a vague recognition, maybe someone I'd seen a few times on the bus or train. The name on the ID card didn't ring a bell at all. Victor Sanz. It wasn't a state-issued ID, though, and there wasn't even a number on it. That had to say something—most likely that he was illegal. The other contents of the wallet weren't helpful either. A CTA card was standard for anyone living in the city. Sixteen dollars in cash was a little odd —I mean why sixteen? What had he bought recently that cost four dollars? Did that mean something? Impossible to tell. Most disturbing, though, was the slip of paper with my address written on it. Unfortunately, there was no other address or social security number I could check into. I just had a face and a name to go on. The cops should be able to figure out who he was faster than I could.

Yeah... the cops.

I hadn't called them yet. I'd have to eventually, but not until I'd thought things through. Obviously, I'd be at the top of the suspect list.

My separation from the CPD wasn't exactly amicable. I'd messed things up pretty bad, pissed a lot of people off, and burned a lot of bridges. Certain individuals still held a grudge and would be thrilled to send me up the river if they got the chance. This would certainly give them the opportunity they were looking for. Of course, if I didn't call them, it would only make me look that much more guilty.

I still had a few friends that wouldn't sell me out, hopefully. My old partner, Jack, was one of them. If I talked to him, he could probably send someone out who didn't have a bone to pick. I'd call him shortly.

The question my brain kept going back to was: who did kill this guy, and why? A number of possibilities came to mind, none any more likely than the next, although one particular scenario demanded serious consideration. What if the killer had been after me? What if it was sheer coincidence that two strangers had been in my flat at the same time and the shooter had assumed this Victor guy was me? Of course, I couldn't answer these questions until I found out who Victor Sanz was and what the hell he was doing in my home to begin with.

This torrent of thoughts and the rain pounding on the window beside me both slowly began to subside. Just as the world gradually became visible through the glass, so too a plan of action took shape. It was fuzzy at first, but grew clearer as my swirling thoughts ebbed to the recesses of my brain. I couldn't see very far ahead, but hopefully, after I'd taken the first few steps, more would reveal itself.

***

I grabbed the phone from its clip on my belt and unlocked it. I'm not sure how people survived before cell phones were invented; I've become inseparable from mine. I've watched scenes in movies where someone chucks their mobile into an ocean or lake and relishes the freedom it brings. I don't buy it for a second. I'd die of a panic attack if somebody did that to me. If I don't want to be bothered, I turn mine off.

Cycling through my contact list, I found the name I was

looking for and hit "send." It rang twice before someone picked up.

"Larsen," said the man on the other end.

"Jack," I said, "It's Gray. I need a favor."

Gray is my last name. I don't give out my first name because it's stupid, and people laugh. See, my mother was an Anglophile, so she named me Earl. As if that's not a god-awful name to begin with, add to it the last name Gray, and... Well, I'm sure you can put it together. My middle name is Mason, same as my old man's. While I don't have anything against him, the name Mason Gray is his, not mine, so I just go by Gray.

"I'll do what I can, Gray, but I'm pretty swamped here. What's going on?" Papers rustled in the background.

Jack and I went back pretty far. We'd gone to school together, taken the same criminal-justice classes. I could tell he was busy by the sound of his voice, but this was important.

"I need you to send an unmarked car to my place. Send the coroner too. And someone to process."

The rustling stopped.

"Gray? What's going on? Are you okay?"

I filled him in with the details and my concerns.

"Okay. I'll do my best to keep it quiet. Is there anything else you want to tell me?"

I knew where he was going with this. "Yeah, take me off the suspect list. The entry wounds are small caliber, probably a . 22. The ME will confirm it. I carry a .380, and that's my only piece."

"Anything else?"

"Yeah. The stiff's name is Victor Sanz. It doesn't ring any bells. The face is familiar, but I can't place it."

"Okay, I'll run it and see if anything pops up. Are you in the apartment?"

"No, I'm at the diner across the street."

7

There was a brief silence. I imagined he was trying to decide if I was serious. Then, "Okay, stay where you are. One of my guys will be there shortly."

"Thanks," I said. Then something else occurred to me, something disturbing. "Jack, one more thing."

"What's that?"

"If somebody is gunning for me, they might go after Frank too. Could you send a squad car over to check on him? Give him the heads up."

"Sure thing. What's the address?" he asked.

"3356 North Seeley," I said. "Over in Roscoe Village."

"Got it," he replied. He reminded me to stay put, and we got off the phone.

I leaned back in the seat and tried to see the next step. Right now, there were too many questions, too many possible causes of my current situation. I needed to narrow them down and focus on one question at a time.

I reached into the inside pocket of my trench coat and took out a notepad and pen—a stereotypical detective accessory, but it's practical. I'm a list man. Some people, like my father, never write anything down. They think it's beneath them. Not me. I use my notepad for everything—grocery lists, to-do lists, facts from interviews, random thoughts, and organizing questions. I've tried using my phone to do it—there are plenty of apps for it —but it's not the same. I'm also aware that my gray trench coat is cliché. That's why I wear it. Like it or not, that's my style.

I started writing down the questions running through my head.

Who was Victor Sanz? The cops were working on that, so I put a "c" beside it.

Who killed him? No way to answer that yet.

Why was he killed? Too many possible answers, but the mistaken identity scenario required that I keep a low profile until I knew the answer.

Why had Victor been in my house? I visualized the scene in my apartment again. Nothing had been broken. No valuables or electronics seemed to have been disturbed, but my desk had been ransacked. Somebody was looking for something, something specific. It could have been Victor or whoever had killed him.

Had they found it? I'd been in such a hurry to get out of the flat I hadn't taken the time to see if anything was missing. I'd have to go back and look. I briefly entertained the idea of dashing across the street to take a quick inventory before the boys in blue showed up, but there wasn't enough time, I decided. If they showed up while I was in there, they'd be pretty pissed. They might even take me in. That wouldn't be good. I might be safe in the slammer, but I sure as hell couldn't get any answers there.

As if to confirm my wise decision, a black Crown Vic with four antennas pulled up in front of the diner, and a suit got out and came through the door. Very subtle. The detective brushed the rain from his shoulders and glanced around the place. Seeing I was the only patron, he walked to my booth and said in a smooth tone, "Mr. Gray?"

I nodded.

"I'm Detective Rowe. Mike Rowe."

I raised my eyebrows.

"No relation," he said flatly.

He slid into the booth across from me and asked about the night's events, so I told him and handed over the dead guy's wallet. Others, he informed me, had parked in the back alley and were processing the scene. He checked my weapon and permit, then handed them back to me and made a note on a pad he'd pulled out while I was telling my story. It was a leather-bound deal, fine-grained, embossed in gold with his last name, with a little elastic loop on the side to hold a pen. A stab of jealousy shot through me. The feeling was stupid, but I couldn't justify dropping twenty bucks on something like that when I could pick up a 4-pack of notepads from the dollar store. Even though I'd love to have something like it, being an independent has its financial limitations. I could feel a divide open between us.

"What time did you arrive at the apartment?" he asked.

I checked my watch. It was straight-up midnight. Damn. How long had I been sitting here? I ran a quick timeline in my head. I'd left the office at eight, met the accountant downtown at eight thirty—that took about an hour—stopped by the store, and then grabbed a cab home. All of which put me home at about...

"Ten... ish."

"Any idea why this guy was in your house?" he asked drolly.

"Nope," I said simply. "I'll let you guys figure that one out." It was just a little fib to keep this guy from interfering in my investigation. Calling Jack was one thing—I knew he'd feed me the info I needed and stay out of my way otherwise—but I didn't know this guy from Adam. Given the reputation of the Chicago Police Department, I figured I'd be better safe than sorry.

"Okay, Mr. Gray," he said. "I don't envy your situation, and I understand your concerns about your... safety."

Crap. I could hear a "but" coming, the inevitable lecture about not interfering with police business. It was now, officially, his investigation. Yadda, yadda, yadda. And then—

"I'm here to help. I'm sure you're aware that we have procedures that must be followed. Certain questions must be asked and answered to clear you as a suspect. I want to make sure that's done as efficiently as possible so that you can proceed with your own affairs. I know you want to solve this puzzle as much as anyone. I only ask that you share whatever you discover with me posthaste. Are we clear?"

I blinked a couple of times as his words sank in. He'd

skipped the lecture and the warnings. He must have known they wouldn't have done any good. Rowe was smarter than he looked: rather than playing the bristling, territorial copper, he was going the route of the sympathetic colleague. Maybe he was sincere, but I didn't buy it.

"Absolutely," I said, and I felt the distance between us widen.

"Good. There's just a few more things we need to take care of: fingerprints and so on. I'll introduce you to the Crime Scene guys. Shall we?"

I nodded. I put a couple of ones on the table to take care of the coffee, then we both stood and walked out into the rain and across the street. Lorraine stood behind the counter, scowling suspiciously at Rowe. Guess she didn't like him any more than I did.

When we arrived in my apartment, three technicians were well into processing the scene for evidence, taking pictures from every angle and dusting my desk for fingerprints. Nothing appeared to have been moved or bagged for evidence yet.

"Once all the pictures have been taken," said the detective, "perhaps you could look through your belongings to tell us if anything is missing."

I was hoping he'd say something like that.

After several minutes, they let me pick through the mess surrounding my desk. Its contents had been rifled through and left lying willy-nilly, but everything appeared to be present and accounted for. Damn, no help there. I gave the detective a shrug.

"All right, Mr. Gray, we've got your number. If we need anything else from you, we'll call. Unfortunately, we can't allow you to remain here. Is there someplace you can stay?"

I thought about it for a few seconds, came up with nothing, and said, "Yeah."

I left the apartment and walked out to the street corner.

2

It was still raining outside, so I stood on the sidewalk under the front awning and waited for it to let up. I wasn't sure what to do next. There was a hotel nearby where I could hole up for the night, and I was pretty tired, but I kept worrying about Frank. Until I heard from Larsen, I wasn't likely to get any sleep. Someone had obviously been looking for something in my apartment, and just as obviously hadn't found it—or had been whacked before they did.

The one solid fact I had was the identity of the dead man, Victor Sanz. Though Larsen was running the name for me, I decided to see what info I could dig up on my own about the guy. The cops might have access to more privileged databases than I did, but they were always short on time and manpower. I might be able to turn something up faster.

Seeing as the weather wasn't about to give me a break, I flipped up the collar on my coat and flagged down the first cab I saw.

Our office is in Old Town—an area right smack between Lincoln Park and the Gold Coast, the two wealthiest neighborhoods in the city. It's also a stone's throw away from Cabrini, one of the poorest. A lot of rich people live in this area: doctors, lawyers, and such. Most of them are north of 40: people with secrets, people with money. It's the perfect spot for a business like ours.

The cabbie dropped me off in front of the brownstone building. I walked the perimeter, checking the second floor for lights. None were on. I made my way up the back stairs and unlocked the door, listening carefully; I wasn't in the mood for any more surprises. The office door was locked and appeared untampered-with. Inside, everything was quiet. Satisfied that no assassins were lurking in the shadows, I sat down at my desk and booted up the computer.

Computers are wonderful things, especially when connected to the Internet. I did most of my work in front of one. Most people think my profession is a thing of the past because any moron can log on and search for whatever they want. This is true, but it takes a lot of time to sift through that much information and find what you're looking for. And time is money. The trick is knowing how and where to look for that needle in the haystack. Plus, a lot of sites require membership fees, which discourages your average Joe. That being said, the Internet is only a starting point. It can help focus your efforts in the field, but real detective work inevitably takes you out of the office and into the brick-and-mortar world.

I started by Googling "Victor Sanz Chicago." 315,000 entries popped up. Great. I hit the images link, which narrowed it down to 200,000, and scrolled down the page. I figured a face would be easier to recognize. Seeing nothing familiar, I narrowed my search even further. A couple of newspaper articles mentioned the name Victor Sanz in connection with alleged thefts, but nothing really stood out. I checked the Cook County Circuit Court site for cases involving a Victor Sanz and came up with the same petty theft records but no convictions.

All the while, I wondered why this guy looked familiar if I didn't know the name. I must have seen him somewhere. But where? On a whim, I checked our in-house database of all the cases we've worked. Maybe I'd met him on an investigation and snapped a few photos of the guy.

I was so intent on my search that I just about crapped myself when the phone buzzed in my pocket. I fished it out hastily, checked the incoming caller id, and swiped my finger across the screen.

"Gray," I said.

"Gray, it's Larsen. Frank's fine—a little irritated at being woken up at one in the morning, but unharmed. The patrolman filled him in on what happened, and he seemed rather baffled. I can't spare a car to post watch, but knowing Frank, he'll take care of it."

"Thanks," I said, and hung up.

I felt better knowing Frank was okay, but now that I was involved in looking for something, I couldn't get any shut-eye until I'd finished the search. Unfortunately, our in-house records turned up nil. At some point, my eyelids got awfully heavy, so I stretched out on the couch in my office to rest them for just a minute.

***

The next thing I knew, sunlight was streaming through the window. I guess it had finally quit raining. But that's not what woke me. I must have heard the front door close in my sleep and decided there might be a threat. Now I heard someone shuffling around outside my office area. I lay very still, slowly reaching for the small semi-automatic pistol at my side. Through my open door, I saw movement across the hall... and then heard whistling to the tune of "Go Tell Aunt Roadie"—well, it was supposed to be. I'm not sure what key it was in, but I did know it was the wrong one.

I immediately relaxed. A morning whistle was one of Frank's annoying little habits. Yesterday's tune had been "What a Friend We Have in Jesus." No telling what he'd come in with tomorrow.

I sat up on the couch and dug something crunchy out of the corner of my left eye. I checked my watch. Eight a.m. I must have groaned, because Frank stuck his head in my door and said, "Oh, morning Gray. Heard you had a rough night. Let me make a pot of coffee, and we'll talk."

I walked over to the bathroom in the hallway, took a leak, and splashed some water on my face. My neck was stiff from

14

sleeping on the couch, and my eyes were bloodshot from lack of sleep. Brad Pitt's got nothing on me in the looks department, I thought.

The coffee brewing down the hall in the kitchenette reached my sniffer, and I felt the drool forming in my mouth. I followed my nose, grabbed a mug off the counter and poured myself a cupful. As I stood there letting the caffeine do its job, Frank wandered around the corner.

"So," he began, "long night?"

A lot of people complain about stupid questions like that. They seem to think that if the answer is obvious, the question needn't be asked. I'm not one of those people, especially in the morning. In fact, I prefer being asked asinine questions that need no real explanation. It requires less thought on my part.

I grunted an affirmative.

"I can only imagine. Listen, I was thinking that you might want a little downtime in the next couple of days. My load is pretty light at the moment, so I can field any new cases and take the ones from yesterday off your hands if you haven't started on them yet."

"That'd be great, Frank. I did interview that accountant last night, but you can have all the others."

"Okay, I'll switch them in the system and you can hand over the files whenever."

"Great," I said. And it was great. I had a feeling that running down this Victor Sanz guy was going to require most of my attention for the next week or so.

Frank went into his office, and I went back to mine. He had assigned me four cases yesterday—the accountant one, a missing person, a premarital screening, and an identity theft—all fairly standard. I pulled the files out of my briefcase, replaced the accountant one, and then made a pile of the others. I checked my watch. It was 9 o'clock on the nose. I took another swallow of coffee, picked up the stack of folders and took them over to Frank.

Dropping the folders on his desk, I said, "I've got a couple of things to look at while I'm here, then I'll take the camera out for a while." I'd made some notes on the accountant's wife's daily schedule; her husband seemed to believe the hanky-panky was happening around lunch time. I figured I'd stake out their neighborhood and see if I could snap a few photos of the adulterous duo. It would also give me time to think of what to do about Victor Sanz.

I went back to my computer and resumed my search. After fifteen fruitless minutes, I was thinking about shutting everything down and heading out when the desk phone intercom thingy rang.

I punched a button. "Yeah."

"Are you sure I gave you this missing person file yesterday?" asked Frank.

"Pretty sure. Why?"

"I can't find it in the computer. You sure it isn't an old case that got mixed in?"

"I don't think so. You want me to see if I can find it on my end?"

"Maybe I just forgot to enter the dad-blamed thing." He was getting a bit forgetful these days, but I remembered seeing it in the system the day before.

"I don't think so. I'll take a look over here. Maybe you've got a glitch."

"Maybe," he said, and hung up.

I opened the database and browsed through the files with yesterday's date on them, but I didn't see the name I was looking for. That was strange. I deleted the date and just ran the name,

Ellie McCarthy. Again, the computer came up with squat.

I walked over to Frank's office.

"Weird, I can't find it either, but I'm positive I saw it yesterday. Let me have a look at the file."

Frank handed it to me. I opened the manila folder and looked over the paperwork. A twenty-one-year-old girl, missing for three weeks, father filed the report, and the cops hadn't turned anything up. It was a typical missing person case, but something tickled the back of my brain.

"I'm gonna hang onto this, Frank. Something's not sitting well. I'm going to head out. If you figure out what's going on with the computer, let me know."

Frank grunted, and I stuffed the McCarthy file into my briefcase, grabbed the camera and made for Lincoln Park.

***

I've had people ask me how I can do a stakeout without a car. Most people think of stakeouts as something that happens late at night, sitting in a black unmarked cruiser while detectives eat crullers and drink scorched corner-store coffee. But what do you expect if they get all their info about law enforcement from reruns of *Cops and Lawyers* or whatever?

The whole point of a stakeout is to watch the target without them knowing that they're being watched. I don't know about you, but if I walked by a car with two people sitting in it with a camera, I'd think something screwy was going on. So I do most of my watching from coffee shops, diners, or cafes. Think about it: when was the last time you paid attention to someone sitting at the Starbucks across the street, even if they did have a camera? Lots of folks carry cameras, and most of them are more interested in taking a black and white photo of the plastic bag that's blown against the fire hydrant because somebody might think it's "artistic" than they are in taking pictures of you. But I digress.

By two o'clock I had plenty of photos of Mrs. Accountant and her new beau, so I figured I'd head downtown and drop off the SD card with Mr. Accountant. I took the El train to the loop, pondering the craziness of the previous night.

The feeling that I'd seen Victor Sanz before wouldn't let go. Why he'd been in my apartment to begin with was, likewise, still a mystery. Add to that the weirdness of the missing file from our database, and my head started to hurt.

The light coming through the windows dimmed as the train went underground. I stared out at the concrete tunnel walls as we sped by, occasionally passing a small access door. I had often wondered what was behind those doors. Was it just a maintenance closet, or was there a network of tunnels webbing their way through the underbelly of Chicago? Did mutant mole people spend the entirety of their blind lives foraging there in the perpetual darkness? I think I read a book about something like that once. Mole people...what an imagination.

Just then, a thought bubbled up through the mire of my brain. I could tell it was something important. I waited for the bubble to reach the surface so I could see it more clearly, and then...

"This is Lake. Doors open on the left at Lake," said the melodious and ambiguously ethnic female voice over the intercom. Crap, this was my stop. I jostled my way out the doors and felt the thought bubble burst. I had no idea what was inside it.

3

After delivering the photos, I paid a visit to the father of our missing girl, Ellie McCarthy, who was also now missing from our database. I dialed the number in the file on the way to the train station. It rang a few times, then a grizzled voice picked up. I told him who I was and that I wanted to come by to talk. He said he'd be there and hung up.

McCarthy lived in Canaryville on the Southside near the old stockyards, the neighborhood made famous by Sinclair's "The Jungle." It's not a place I go very often; I generally stick to the north side of the city, because that's where my business is. Don't get me wrong, there are some affluent areas on the south side, but not nearly as many as north of the loop. Also, I kind of stick out down there.

Few people are "from" Chicago itself: we're mostly transplants from other places. Generally when someone tells you they're from Chicago, they mean one of the surrounding suburbs. Neighborhoods like Canary Park and Bridgeport, however, are some of the few places people are actually "from." With a long history in the city, they maintain a strong sense of community, and outsiders simply don't fit in—and if your grandparents didn't grow up there, you're an outsider.

McCarthy's house was a small bungalow typical of the neighborhood. As his name would suggest, he was thoroughly Irish, like most of the folks there.

The Irish in urban areas of America have gotten a raw deal over the last couple centuries, stereotyped by Hollywood as bigoted and hot-tempered. What many people don't realize, or choose to ignore, is that like many ethnic minorities, they were oppressed and taken advantage of in the early years of our nation's history. They weren't slaves, by any means, but they did endure horrid conditions.

McCarthy didn't exude any of the stereotypical anger, re-sentment, or animosity usually attributed to such people. In-stead, he was blanketed by an aura of deep sadness. He was most likely in his late fifties, but he looked older: his full head of hair was snowy white, and there were deep creases around his mouth and eyes. The last couple of weeks obviously weighed heavily on him.

After letting me in, he walked to a small corner table in the living room, poured two fingers of Glenlivet into a tumbler, and handed it to me. Though not my typical drink, I graciously accepted. Then he poured a second glass for himself.

We settled on the couch, then I spoke up. "I've got a copy of the police report you filed last week, but I was hoping to get a more personal sense for your daughter. What can you tell me about her? What are her hobbies? Where does she spend her free time?"

He sat quietly for a moment, then said, "I'm not sure what I can tell you. We've grown apart the last several years. I don't know much about her personal life anymore. We used to be bud-dies. We'd go bowling, go to the movies. After her mother died, I'd take her down to the pub with me, and she'd tell me all about her dreams while I had a pint. She always wanted to be an archi-tect, and she'd draw me sketches of what the city skyline would look like when she got through with it. But when she went to col-lege, I started seeing less and less of her until she finally got a place of her own closer to downtown.

"She always called me every Monday, though. That's how I knew something was wrong—she didn't call the other week."

"What about friends? Did she ever talk about the people she spent time with?"

"Not really—not to me, anyway. I got the feeling there

was somebody, a boyfriend maybe, but she never did talk about him outright. She would mention things she had done, places she'd gone, that wouldn't be right to do alone. I don't know... it seemed like she wanted to keep me in the dark where that was concerned."

"All right. These places she went, do you remember where they were? Any place she mentioned more than once?"

"Not really. Mostly restaurants. There was a club she went to a couple of times. Some place called Neo. You know that one?"

"Yeah, I've heard of it," I replied.

Neo is the oldest nightclub in Chicago. There are older bars and speakeasies in the city, such as the Green Mill, one of Capone's favorite hangouts, but that's a different type of place altogether. Neo plays host to goths, emo kids, and anyone else who wears a lot of black, and it's one of the few places in the city that plays trip-hop music. I've never been there, but it looked like that was about to change.

"What about social media? Does she use that much?"

McCarthy met my question with a blank stare.

"Computers. Does she have one?"

"Huh? Oh yeah. She's been trying to talk me into getting one, but I'm one of the last geezers to hold out, I guess."

I didn't think the old man would provide any more insight into the whereabouts of his daughter, so I thanked him for his time, confirmed Ellie's address, polished off the last swig of whiskey, and said my farewell.

***

As I headed back to the Red Line, I passed a billboard near the Sox field that stopped me short, an ad for someone named Dooley running for alderman of the 3rd ward. That, of itself, was meaningless to me, but it's funny how the brain works, how one thought connects to another. I'd read in a book that certain external stimuli can unearth buried memories if they somehow trigger the right synapses in the brain to fire, no matter how meaningless those stimuli might seem at first. Somehow, seeing this billboard sent me down a pathway of synapses that ended at a gala I had attended a year ago, hosted by a different alderman in another ward.

I'd figured this reception, held so the locals could meet the alderman on a non-threatening level with no agendas being pushed, was a good opportunity for me to schmooze and possibly drum up some new clients. There'd been a buffet of finger foods and a mimosa bar, but my brain freeze-framed on the face of none other than Victor Sanz. Ha! I knew I'd seen him before. In my mind's eye, he was dressed in a white uniform, filling champagne flutes with orange juice.

I did a little shuffle step on the sidewalk and lit a cigarette to celebrate this victory. I know, it doesn't seem like much, but in my line of work, it's often the little things that count the most. They add up to big breakthroughs.

I also now knew the next step in my investigation: to talk to the folks at the alderman's office. Either Sanz worked directly for them or for the caterer who'd worked the event. Either way, there would be paperwork with an address or something. I fished out my notepad, wrote this down, and made for the train.

4

Once the train resurfaced, I looked up the ward office I needed and dialed the number.

"Thank you for calling the office of Alderman Juarez," chirped a female voice on the other end. "How may I help you?"

I told her I was a PI trying to track down someone named Victor Sanz who'd worked an event there earlier in the year and asked if she would be so kind as to check the records for me. She put me on hold, forcing me to listen to terrible Muzak. You'd think that with Pandora and Sirius and all the other on-demand technology these days, someone would have figured out a way to make hold music less boring. A few moments later, the receptionist came back on line and ever so politely informed me that the event I was referring to had been catered in-house, but there were no records of anyone by that name having worked there. She was "very sorry she couldn't be of more help" and "hoped that I would have a nice day."

Huh. That sure seemed like a dead end—except I knew better. Her tone had the cold detachment of someone stonewalling. I knew it well; all receptionists used it when they had been instructed by a boss to "tell that damned PI to go to hell." I was more than a little surprised to be stonewalled so early, though; I'd honestly expected it to be a simple exchange of information. Something was afoot.

Naturally, this required me to make the poor receptionist uncomfortable by showing up in person. Oftentimes, those nice young girls couldn't brush me off so easily face-to-face. A lot depended on how much experience they had and how willing they were to protect their douche bag boss. Fortunately, the ward office was just off the Red Line, and I didn't have anything better to do.

Switching my train of thought, I opened Facebook on my phone and searched for Ellie McCarthy. Her father might not know how to use this newfangled electronic stuff to keep tabs on his daughter, but I certainly did. It didn't take long to find her page, but it wasn't much help. Her last activity had been six months prior, and her privacy settings were locked down tight. The only things I could get to were her profile picture and basic info. At least the photo was more recent than the one in my file.

Ellie was a pretty girl. She had a thick mane of dark red hair rebelling against the clips that struggled to hold it in check. Her face was round—not plump, exactly, but healthy. The Irish freckle fairy had given her a liberal dusting across her cheeks and long, high-bridged nose, setting a stark contrast to the creamy white skin beneath. The camera had caught her laughing, and her bright green eyes danced with joy and innocence.

While I was thinking about the McCarthy file, I called Frank to see about the computers. He still hadn't figured out what happened on his end: the file simply wasn't there. I told Frank I knew a guy who might be able to help.

Next I called Mac. Mac's real name was Keith, I think. Maybe Kevin. I don't remember. I met him on a case in which I'd recovered a damaged hard drive for a client. There was some-thing about the case that didn't sit right with me so I wanted to know what was on the drive before I handed it over. Mac had a computer repair shop in the neighborhood, so I took it over to see if he could do anything with it. Turned out he was a genius with anything that spoke a language of ones and zeros, except he refused to work on any Apple products—he'd apparently been let go from the company over a security breach that he swore he had nothing to do with. I found his vehement denial dubious. Calling him Mac seemed the only natural, if somewhat mean-spirited, thing to do.

Anyway, he'd salvaged the data from the hard drive, and

we'd discovered some adult video footage. Because it was, in fact, all adult, I saw no reason not to return it to the client. Ever since then, Mac has been my go-to guy for all things technology.

"Hey Mac," I said, "its Gray. I've got a job for you."

"I've told you I don't like that name. Why do you insist?"

"I don't know. Irony?"

He didn't laugh.

"Do you have time to swing by my office and take a look at our system?" I asked. "Something wiggy is going on."

"What kind of wiggy?"

I told him about the missing file and that I was primarily interested in how it disappeared rather than in getting it back. "I'm not in the office, but Frank should be."

"Can it wait until tomorrow? It's almost quitting time," Mac said.

"Charge me for overtime" I said. "It's important."

He groaned. "Fine. I'll be there shortly."

"Thanks," I said, and hung up. I called Frank to let him know Mac would be stopping by, then got ready to hop off the train as we approached my stop.

***

The Alderman's office wasn't huge. Of course, it wasn't a huge ward either. It was practical—plain painted walls, plain office-store-type furniture, plain receptionist sitting behind the desk—not what you'd expect in a Chi-town politico's office. But then again, we weren't downtown, where most of the money and power is.

I sidled up to the desk of the receptionist, who was on the phone. She held up a finger as if to say "I'll be with you in a moment," and I flashed her a smile that said "I've got all day." She was a young Hispanic girl, probably in her mid-twenties, with thick brown hair. She wasn't what I'd call pretty, but she wasn't ugly either—unremarkable, I guess you'd say.

She hung up the phone, then asked, "How can I help you?"

"I'm here to see Mr. Juarez," I told her.

"Do you have an appointment?"

"Do I need one? I'm a constituent of this ward."

"I'm sorry sir, but Mr. Juarez is very busy at the moment. I'd be happy to make an appointment for you."

"All right, then. My name is Gray." I had no intention of making an appointment. I did, however, intend on making a scene until I got some information, and this was part one of the plan.

"Okay, Mr. Gray. What will be the nature of your meeting, so Mr. Juarez will be prepared?"

Time to make her uncomfortable. "I'd like to speak with him about a man named Victor Sanz."

Her demeanor instantly changed from warm to wary. If I was right about being stonewalled, she wouldn't simply make me an appointment now, but neither could she outright refuse to make one—politics, you know. On the other hand, if she had told me the truth on the phone, she would make the appointment and let the alderman tell me again.

"One moment, please. I need to check with his assistant to see when he is available." She punched a few buttons on the phone, avoiding eye contact, then spoke into the handset, "Yes, a gentleman named Mr. Gray is inquiring about a Victor Sanz and would like to make an appointment." A pause, then, "Uh huh. Thank you. I'll let him know." She hung up the phone. "You can have a seat over there. Someone will be with you shortly."

That was unexpected.

Perhaps this was a different tactic, a wait-'em-out game. They'd feign an interest in what I wanted, then leave me sitting in the lobby for hours, saying "It will just be a few more minutes" every so often until I got frustrated and left or the office closed.

I was wrong again. Within ten minutes, a young, dark--haired fellow with a sharp beak of a nose came down the hall-way. He wore khaki slacks, a blue JC Penny button-up, and a bow tie. Seriously, a bow tie. Apparently, they're making a comeback with the twenty-somethings.

"Good afternoon, Mr. Gray," he began. "I'm Jason Gal-lagher, Mr. Juarez's personal assistant." He extended his right hand and, on reflex, I shook it. I felt something stick me in the palm when I did, but before I could pull away, he grabbed my hand with his left in a firm two-handed shake before continuing to speak. "I'm very sorry that Mr. Juarez couldn't speak with you personally about your issue at this time. Please know that your concerns are our concerns..."

I stopped listening, trying to figure out what was poking me in the hand. It wasn't a needle or blade, as I'd initially feared. It was softer and had more give to it, like the edge of a business card. In fact, I concluded, that's exactly what it was. That was very odd. Truthfully, this whole encounter was odd.

"... I hope you understand, and we thank you for your con-tinued support." When he finished, he gave my hand two hard shakes and made sure I kept my fist balled around whatever it was. He stared at me, searching my eyes to see if I did actually understand.

My neurons fired off along a hundred different pathways as I considered the implications. The card in my hand could have absolutely nothing on it—it could be just another ploy to get rid of me. Maybe they figured if I walked out the door, I would be re-luctant to come back in and make a stink. It was also possible that Victor Sanz's address was written on this card, but no one wanted to admit that he was connected to the office. That would make sense: what politician wants to deal with the murder of a staff member? Whatever was on this card was intended to remain a secret.

I thought about looking at the card then and there to thumb my nose at "the man" —I couldn't care less about Mr. Juarez's political machinations. Then I thought about the mistaken identity scenario I'd come up with earlier. If someone wanted me dead, I probably shouldn't antagonize them.

Caution won out, and I mumbled, "Sure... sure, no problem."

The assistant released me but maintained eye contact until I turned and walked to the door. I nodded to the receptionist, who gave me a trite smile, then looked back over my shoulder. Mr. Gallagher had already disappeared down the hallway.

I waited until I was halfway to the El before looking at the crumpled piece of cardstock still clutched in my fist. Sure enough, it was a business card for Alderman Juarez. I flipped it over and read the hastily scribbled note: *Carol's 9:30.*

5

My watch said it was five thirty, and I hadn't eaten lunch yet, so I stopped off at Duck Walk, my favorite little Thai place in Lincoln Park. Honestly, I liked it better when it was a hole in the wall up in Lakeview off the Belmont stop. It was super cheap and it only sat eight or so people, but the food was fan-freaking-tastic. The new location is a little swankier, and they've raised the prices some, but the grub is the same. For the urban gastronomist the Tom Kha soup is ambrosia- or amrita, the Buddhist equivalent, if you want to get technical about it. The sweet coconut milk base is the perfect palette on which the heat of crushed red peppers, the zing of fresh ginger, and the tang of lime mingle to create a tempting tableaux of taste. None of this has any bearing on the case, of course, but it provided me with a needed break so I could focus on the simple pleasures of life.

After that I grabbed a cab and went back to the office.

Some people don't believe in luck; they think it's only a function of opportunity and preparedness. Some people don't believe in coincidence; they claim all occurrences are part of a grand design. Me, I think it's just a matter of semantics; the end result is the same. But whatever you want to call it, it worked in my favor that day.

Here's what happened as best as I can recall.

I went up the back way to the office again. Like many other multi-unit buildings in Chicago, the back of our building has a wooden staircase that leads to a landing at each floor. These landings always have a handrail of some kind; ours had a solid plywood enclosure about waist high.

I pulled my keys out as I reached the landing and was about to unlock the door when I felt a ten-pound furball brush against my legs. I glanced down at our resident alley cat, One-eyed Willy, and said hi. Apparently, verbal recognition wasn't enough, because he let out a loud growling meow. I knelt down to scratch him behind his scarred and mangled ear.

That timing saved my life.

As soon as I moved, I heard a *thwack* on the wall where my head had been. Several tiny stone chips rained down on me. I immediately dropped to my stomach, and Willy took off.

Someone had just taken a shot at me.

Though the plywood wall would offer no protection from a normal round of ammunition, I hoped it would be shield enough from the type my attacker was using, since there'd been no audible crack to accompany the gunshot.

Many people believe that a silencer on the end of a barrel literally silences the gunshot or converts it into a high-pitched *fffttt* sound. That isn't true. The reason a gunshot is so loud is because the bullet travels faster than the speed of sound, creating a sonic boom. The only way to silence a gunshot is to slow the bullet. That's not usually possible, but there is one way: a low-velocity .22-caliber ammunition on the market which effectively makes a .22 rifle no louder than a BB gun. It's highly illegal in most states, but when has that ever stopped a would-be criminal?

Those slowed-down bullets might penetrate plywood, but they'd lose most of their energy in doing so. Lying prone, I should be safe for the time being, but I couldn't stay like that forever.

I considered my options.

I could draw my own piece and return fire, but I only had a vague idea of the assailant's position. By the time I zeroed in on him, I'd be dead.

I could try to unlock the door and get inside. I glanced up at the lock. It was above the protection of the wall. That was no good either: my head would be exposed.

I had my phone, so I could call the cops. Any normal person would. The problem with that was that it could take them twenty minutes to get there, and if this assassin really wanted me dead, he'd finish me off before that. I needed to get to a safer position first.

I decided to call the office. If Frank was there, he could open the door from inside.

The phone rang seven times, then the voice mail picked up. Shit.

My mind scrabbled like a frantic hamster on a wheel as I tried to find a way out, then froze on a scene from the front of the building when the cabbie dropped me off. A powder blue Beetle had been parked on the side street—the same car that Mac drove. He must be inside, working on the computer issue. Perfect.

I dialed Mac's cell. He picked up on the second ring.

"Computer 911," he said. "If you've got a problem, I've got the solution."

"Good, 'cause I've got one hell of a problem."

"Oh, hi, Gray. I'm glad you called. I found something—"

"Not now," I interrupted. "I need you to do exactly what I say, and I need you to do it now."

"Okay..."

"Come to the back door, but stay away from the windows. Whatever you do, don't stand or walk in front of them."

"Shit, Gray, you're scaring me. What's going on?"

"I'll tell you in a minute. Right now, just follow my directions."

"Okay, I'm at the back door. Now what?"

"In a second, you're going to open the door, but make sure you're standing behind it. I'm going to somersault in, and as soon as I'm clear, you close the door. Got it?"

"I think so."

"Good. On the count of three." I gathered my legs underneath me and prepared to launch myself through the opening. "One, two, three."

The deadbolt turned, and the door swung open. Mac must have followed my directions, because I couldn't see him. I leapfrogged in, pushing off with both my arms and my legs. It wasn't graceful, and fell far short of a somersault, but it got me in. When my hands hit the floor inside, I pulled up my legs and half rolled, half scrambled far enough in that Mac could slam the door behind me.

Once the door was closed, I clambered to my feet and locked it. I rushed to the front door and secured it as well, leaving Mac slack-jawed with confusion in my wake. We had a few windows in the office, but most were obscured by blinds. As long as we stayed clear of the ones that weren't, we should be okay.

Now that I was reasonably safe from sniper fire, I dialed Frank's cell phone and left a detailed message as to why he might want to take the next day off. Next, I called the boys in blue. I figured that a few uniforms crawling around the place might deter the shooter from hanging around for another shot when I left.

"Sorry about that, Mac," I said when I hung up. Mac, with his wiry frame, short black beard, and stainless steel barbell through his eyebrow, still looked dazed and confused. "I guess I owe you an explanation."

"That would be nice."

"To make a long story short, somebody is trying to kill me. They had me pinned down out on the back balcony."

"Seriously? That's heavy. Why?"

"I'm not sure, but I think it has something to do with that file I asked you to look into. You said you found something?"

"Yeah, let me show you." Now that we were back in his comfort zone, the shock was wearing off. He led me back to my computer; I checked each room before we entered to make sure we wouldn't present targets.

"There's actually no trace of that file anywhere, which is unusual, because even when you delete something, remnants always linger on your hard drive," he explained. "If this file was ever on your system, then somebody did a bang-up job of scrubbing it."

"So if it's completely gone, what did you find?"

"That's where this gets interesting. I found a piece of code that looks like some sort of spyware."

"Like a virus?" I asked, hoping I didn't sound like a complete idiot.

"Kind of," he replied. "Spyware doesn't do any damage on its own, though, and it isn't designed to replicate and spread to other computers like a virus does."

"Okay, so what *does* it do?"

"In layman's terms, it creates a door that a hacker can use to access your system without your knowledge. In this case, I think it was used to delete your file."

"Okay, so what next? Is there any way to trace the spyware like they do in the movies?"

"That depends on how the spyware got onto your system. If it came through an email or a website, maybe. If it was installed manually with a flash drive or CD, then no."

"How can you figure that out?" I asked.

"Time," he replied with a sigh, "and a lot of searching."

6

The ornate mahogany doors, framed in hand-carved reliefs of biblical angels and demons, swung open, revealing a truly opulent office. Its expanse of black marble floor was interrupted only by an ancient Persian rug, behind which sat a desk the color of obsidian. The only thing more impressive was the bird's-eye view, seen through the floor-to-ceiling, wall-to-wall windows directly behind it, of the city sprawled below.

Even though he had been in this office hundreds of times, Michael couldn't help but be awed by the vista, especially at this time of night, with all the lights twinkling below, the headlights of thousands of people driving to and from whatever menial activities occupied their existence.

Facing the windows was the one who had summoned him here. There were many powerful people living in this city— Michael dealt with most of them on a regular basis—but none had the sheer presence of this one. He wore a gray pinstripe wool suit. Most would call his features attractive, but not exceptionally so.

"Magnificent, isn't it?"

The voice filled Michael with ten thousand emotions all at once, as nothing else could; joy, excitement, pride, fear, apprehension, relief, envy, hope, and admiration washed over him. It had taken him years to learn how not to be swept away by them, how to maintain mental focus and stand firm in the incessant tide. That was why he had attained his position, why he was here now. Very few others could keep their sense of self in this one's presence.

"Indeed," answered Michael, "it is."

"There is a situation. You know of the rebels?"

"If you mean the group calling themselves Red Dread, then yes."

"I've been tolerant of their foolishness, have I not?"

"You have."

"But they have made a dire mistake—one that will have serious consequences."

"It is time to remove them?"

The one spun to face Michael. "M'Hael!"

The use of his proper name startled Michael. It had been so long since anyone had called him that. Coming from this one's lips, it was more than he could take. Michael collapsed to one knee.

Stupid. Such an order would have to come from the Circle itself. He was dangerously close to overstepping his bounds.

"My apologies," Michael stammered.

"You are forgiven. It has come to my attention that this... Red Dread," he said with disgust, "have availed themselves of a certain asset to deal with a potential threat. It is well within my power to nullify their contract with that asset and prevent them from using any of our other resources. Should this threat deal with our upstarts himself, the Circle need not be disturbed. Contact Harrison. Instruct him to stand down. Make sure everyone knows our stance on doing business with this group."

"Yes sir," Michael replied. "It shall be so."

As Michael quietly closed the door, Mr. Monday turned back to the window, once more admiring his domain.

7

Carol's Pub is a seedy little dive bar in my neighborhood, the only place I know of in the city that caters to the country and western crowd. It's a scene straight out of *Road House*. The bouncer is a burly fellow with a long black beard and a ponytail who wears a leather biker jacket and sunglasses at eleven p.m. It even has chicken wire wrapped around the stage where the band plays. All that's missing is Patrick Swayze and a blind keyboard player.

I got there about eight thirty so I could find a seat with a good view of the door. I really didn't want anyone sneaking up on me here.

Mac and I had waited at the office until the cops showed up. While I filed a report and gave my statement, I had Mac pack up my computer so he could take it back to his shop to keep working. I didn't feel comfortable leaving him alone at the office after what happened, and this way he could work on it through the night. I also swapped the trench coat and fedora for a ball cap and windbreaker out of the closet so I wouldn't be such a sore thumb. I helped Mac load the computer into the car while the officers bumbled their way through possible trajectories and dug mutilated slugs out of the wall, then Mac dropped me off at the train.

Sitting at this tiny table for two in this smoky little joint watching for someone I'd never met to show up and hopefully give me information I desperately wanted set my mind to buzzing. By now, I was certain that Victor Sanz had simply been in the wrong place at the wrong time and that two attempts had been made to end me in the last two days. My gut told me it was connected to the McCarthy case, but I had no real proof other than a deleted file. I racked my brain, thinking who else might want me dead. I mean, I've ended a lot of marriages, ruined a couple of careers, and pissed off several people over the years, but I couldn't imagine any of them hiring a hit man to come after me. One thing was sure: I needed to be a lot more careful if I planned on making it through the week.

I fingered Alderman Juarez's business card and studied my fellow patrons. There weren't many at this hour—the live music didn't start until ten—but four men and one woman, not including the bartenders, appeared to be getting an early start on the night's drinking. They were all at the bar, though one sat apart from the others at the end.

I eyed them closely, noting their clothing. All wore jeans, and the lady, a too-tight tube top. Two of the men were in cow-boy boots. One of the gents wore a white T-shirt, and I noticed a crude tattoo peeking out of his sleeve. Could be a prison job. I'd keep an eye on him.

Christ. I was getting paranoid. Careful was one thing, but paranoid could get me killed. It had a habit of filling your head so full of imagined threats that you didn't notice the real ones sneaking up behind you.

I flagged down the only waitress and ordered a gin and tonic to settle my thoughts. Drink in hand, I refocused on the body language of the patrons.

Clothing tells you what a person wants you to think about them, but body language tells you what they think of themselves. The woman sat with her shoulders hunched, indicating low self-esteem, but she was trying to compensate by being overly touchy with the men sitting next to her. One of them was repulsed, as evidenced by the angle of his body. The other was trying to ig-nore the woman's advances by facing the bar straight on with his shoulders, but his legs and hips were turned slightly toward her. Tattoo-boy at the end was slouched and hunched, nursing his beer. He looked deflated, defeated. He didn't seem to be a threat after all.

About ten till, another pair walked through the door. The first was an imposing figure—a coiled spring of tension, eyes darting from face to face, searching out the dark corners of the bar for any threat. He, too, wore a light windbreaker, the faint outline of a sidearm concealed within. I could tell immediately the second was the alderman. Despite the relaxed-fit jeans, rumpled T-shirt, and Cubs cap he wore in an effort to dress down, his posture and gait screamed power. He was a good-looking guy of some Latino or Hispanic descent; Puerto Rican was my guess. His eyes flicked nervously around the bar, and the corners of his mouth were drawn with worry.

The others patrons looked up at the newcomers, but broke eye contact immediately, too intimidated to risk any interaction. The alderman's gaze slid over to me, and we locked eyes. I nodded. He put his hand on the other man's shoulder and said something in his ear. The bodyguard, as I presumed, then took a seat at a table near the door and Juarez walked over to my table.

"Mr. Gray?" he inquired, looming over me.

"Alderman."

He sat down in the chair opposite me.

"I'd like to apologize for the clandestine nature of our meeting. As I'm sure you can imagine, there are certain things we might discuss tonight that my opponents would want to use against me. But in light of last night's happenings, I feel I owe you an explanation."

Ya think. "I'd appreciate that," I said. I decided to get right to the point. "So you are familiar with Victor Sanz, I take it."

"Yes. We were good friends when I was younger. He helped me through some difficult times in high school. Unfortunately, our paths diverged, and he ran into troubles of his own. As I climbed from the mire of the city streets, I hoped to make an honest man of him. I provided legal counsel several years ago when he ran afoul of the law, and since then, he has tried to do right by me. I've given him work when and where I could, and until now I have not regretted it."

"Why was he in my apartment?"

"The last time I saw him, I asked him to find out what you knew, without divulging my identity, about a case of yours. It was not my intent that he break into your home. I should have been clearer in my instructions.

"You're saying Sanz broke into my apartment to find one of my case files as a favor to you?"

"So it would appear."

"But you didn't actually tell him to break in?"

"Absolutely not," he replied.

"Plausible deniability, eh?" I couldn't help poking the bear. Politicians chapped my ass. They played by a different set of rules than everyone else and usually got away with some pretty sketchy stuff. He didn't laugh.

"As I said Mr. Gray, I was trying to make an honest man out of Victor. I had hoped he would simply speak with you about the matter in confidence. In hindsight, it seems obvious that he would have interpreted my words to suggest an illicit action, given his prior offenses. But I did not see it that way at the time. His death is and always will be on my conscience." The alderman sighed deeply as the burden settled about his shoulders.

"Fair enough," I said, cutting him some slack. He'd given me new questions that now needed answers. "Which case of mine are you so interested in?"

"Ellie's." He said the name so softly and with such tenderness that it caught me off guard. *Ellie? Ellie who?* "Wait, the McCarthy case?"

He nodded.

The questions raced through my head and jammed like a multi car pile-up on the expressway. I had to slow down, organize my thoughts. One question at a time.

"Why do you want to know about that one?" I asked, leaning forward.

He paused, trying to figure out how to answer, then said, "She's my girlfriend."

"I see." I leaned back and laced my fingers behind my head. "So why all the cloak and dagger? Wouldn't anyone be worried about their significant other?"

"It's a bit more complicated than that," he began, then paused to flag down the waitress and ordered an Old Style. *Gross.*

"How do you mean?"

"Politics," he chuffed.

"You're gonna have to explain that."

"One's choice of life partner can have huge repercussions on a political career. It may not matter to you, but an up and coming Latino such as myself getting involved with an Irish girl from Canary Park is a big deal to a lot of people. It can either build bridges or destroy them, depending on who spins it and how. Plus, an alderman's girlfriend can fall under a lot of pressure. Ellie wasn't sure she wanted to deal with all of that yet, so we chose to keep our relationship secret until... for the time being."

I wanted to despise Juarez and all that he stood for, but instead I realized what I really despised was the nature of politics itself. Him, I just felt sorry for. He seemed like a decent guy with solid values, but his actions and decisions were warped by the game he played in an attempt to make a difference. No one should have to hide their relationships and feelings from the ever-watching public eye.

"How did you know I had been hired to investigate her disappearance?" It bugged me that he'd found out so fast. The alderman leaned back in his seat and laced his fingers behind his head. Just then, the waitress came with the alderman's beer and set it in front of him. When she had returned to the bar, he said, "The same way I found out that Victor had been murdered. Politics." He smiled.

I knew I wouldn't get anything more specific out of him. Even I don't talk about my sources. The alderman was obviously connected—probably to the PD, maybe to other people and places as well. Phone taps were a possibility, likely on Ellie's old man's, since he was the one who'd hired us. Anyway, the specifics didn't really matter.

"All right, Mr. Juarez." I shifted again and placed my elbows on the table. "Let's say the break-in was a mistake. That still doesn't explain why Sanz is dead. Can you shed any light on that? Could he have been followed by any of your enemies, or did he have any of his own?"

"Good question. I doubt I have made any enemies, as of yet, who would kill an errand boy to spite me. As for enemies of his own, he most certainly had them. However, this appears to have been a professional job, and most of Victor's enemies wouldn't be capable of such a thing. If they wanted him dead, they would have done it differently, most likely a face-to-face confrontation, so he would know who was responsible, or perhaps a drive-by if brevity was desired. This kind of calculated killing hints at a different mindset. I will, however, be asking some very pointed questions to certain parties from Victor's past. Just to be sure." He took a long pull from his glass.

"That sounds... interesting." *Creepy, but I'd like to see it.* Apparently Mr. Juarez had no qualms about going up against gangs and drug dealers, and it sounded like he didn't follow the rules when doing so, either. Maybe I could like this guy after all.

"So..." he drawled.

"So..." I drawled back. I had more questions, but to keep the conversation balanced, I needed him to ask the next one.

"What *can* you tell me about Ellie?" he finally ventured.

"Probably less than you already know. I only started my investigation today. The police file was skimpy. I spoke with her father, but he doesn't know much, though he did give me one lead."

"What sort of lead?" Juarez's eyes suddenly sharpened.

"It's pretty thin. He said she'd mentioned the club Neo a couple of times. Do you know anything about that?" Right now, Juarez was the best lead I had. He hadn't spoken with the cops, and I'd bet a Benny he knew something that would help.

His eyes moved back and forth as he accessed his internal database.

"She mentioned going there a few times. Said she liked the atmosphere, that it was a good escape from reality. That's about it."

"You never went with her?"

"No."

"Why would your girlfriend go to a nightclub without you?"

"Because our relationship was so secretive, and because I work late a lot, she had a life outside of us. I wasn't threatened by it," he said, not in the least defensive, simply explaining the facts.

"Hang on a second," I said, fishing around for my notepad and pen. "When did you see her last?"

"The day before she went missing, I think. We had dinner on Thursday three weeks ago."

"Where?"

"Sai Cafe. It's a sushi place just off Fullerton." I jotted this down in my notebook while he continued. "My schedule was full on Friday, so we'd planned to get together on Saturday. That morning, she didn't answer the phone. I'm sure I called ten times that day and twenty on Sunday, but everything went straight to voice-mail. I was beside myself with worry. I didn't know what to do, or if I should file a missing-person report myself. After all,

I'm not family. No one knew we were dating."

"What about those contacts at the PD? Couldn't you have asked them to look into it?"

"Hindsight, Mr. Gray. If I had thought about it at the time, I certainly would have. Once her father filed the report, I came to my senses and did just that."

Check. I was right about those contacts, after all.

"So why isn't there more in the official file? I've seen several missing person reports over the years, and this one seems lacking, like someone wasn't taking it seriously."

Juarez sank back into his seat. "I know. It has me worried."

This just got more interesting.

"You think someone is intentionally not looking?"

"Maybe. I certainly expected more." He didn't want to make outright accusations, but I could tell his mind was headed into dark territory. I decided to go along for the trip.

"A cover-up, then?"

Juarez steepled his fingers.

Oh boy. Let the conspiracy theories commence.

I waited a moment to see what else he would say, but he wasn't ready yet. I needed to prod him a little more. He was close to telling me something important.

"The police report says there were no keys, purse, or phone in her apartment, that she might have chosen to disappear."

"I don't buy it," he said. "She had no reason to, as far as I know. I'm certain she would have said something to me or her father if she'd planned on dropping off the grid."

"That's what I was thinking," I confirmed. "This doesn't feel like a runaway case. What do you think might have happened?"

"It's not what I think. It's what I'm afraid of."

"What are you afraid of, then?"

"Human trafficking," he said in a hushed tone.

"Really?"

"You think I'm kidding."

"Well, it's not something I had considered. I thought that mostly happened in other countries."

He grunted. "Yes, the media loves to talk about the horrors that happen in other places. No one likes to admit that such things can happen in their own backyard. But they do. Do you know how many people are reported missing every day?"

"Not really," I admitted.

"Around 2,500. Every day."

"That many?"

"Frightening, isn't it? Granted, most of them are runaways or people trying to get lost. Only a handful have been kidnapped or murdered. But what's really scary is how many missing people are never reported. Homeless people, runaways, drug addicts, prostitutes. People who have fallen through all of our society's safety nets. These are the people the traffickers target, because no one looks for them. But once in a while the traffickers make a mistake and take the wrong person, and that person usually ends up dead. That's what I'm afraid of, Mr. Gray."

I took a moment to digest all of this.

"Do these slave traders have a presence in Chicago?"

"Most assuredly."

"Do you have any proof?"

Juarez pressed his lips together and shook his head. "Nothing solid. Just back alley whisperings and reports from a source that keeps me in touch with the streets."

"So there's no reason for the cops to go in that direction."

"Even if there were some piece of evidence I could give them, I'm not sure it would do any good."

I arched an eyebrow at this, then tried to predict his logic.

"Politics, right?" He smirked. "Let me guess. Doing so would stir up the muck at the bottom of the pond, and no one wants to get the whole pond dirty. As long as the muck stays at the bottom where no one can see it, everyone's happy to leave it alone."

"Something like that."

"But you're hoping that Mr. Private Eye here will look into it... and maybe come up with a handful of mud that you can sling at an opponent when the time is right." I really hated politicians.

"My priority is finding Ellie," he retorted. "Whatever else you uncover is incidental, even if its discovery would be for the greater good."

"I've already been hired to find Miss McCarthy. If you want me to find information on this human trafficking ring, that's certainly negotiable."

"Fair enough." Juarez slid a folded piece of paper across the table. "That's the name of my source and the address where you should be able to find him. Play nice, and maybe he can give you more information."

I took the paper, quickly read the name—Jimmy Armstrong—and stuck it in my pocket.

"One more question," I said. "How good are you with computers?"

"Good enough to send an email and type up a document. Beyond that, my assistant handles everything."

"That would be Mr. Gallagher?"

Juarez nodded.

"Is he aware of your relationship status?"

"Yes. He's the only one on my staff who knows."

"I see. I'll need to speak with him again."

"Oh. I hadn't thought... Yes, that can be arranged," he said, blinking at the thought that one of his staff could be involved.

"Good. Is there anything else that you think might be helpful in finding Miss McCarthy?"

"I wish I knew something else. Just, please, be discreet in your investigation. I'd hate for something terrible to happen to Ellie because her disappearance became a high-profile case."

"You have my word, Mr. Juarez, that her safety is my utmost concern. I'll do whatever it takes to bring her home, if that's at all possible."

"Thank you." He stood, placed a ten-dollar bill on the table, and offered me his hand. "I'll set up a time for you to speak with Jason at your earliest convenience. And again, I'm truly sorry for what happened at your apartment." He looked as if he was about to say something more, but stopped himself. We shook hands, then he turned and nodded at his escort, who joined him immediately, and they both left.

I stared after them for a bit, mulling over this new information. Ten minutes later, I knocked back the last of my cocktail and paid my tab, then decided I had one more stop to make before calling it a night.

8

On the way to Lincoln Park, I called Mac.

"No, I haven't found anything yet," he huffed when he picked up.

"Wasn't expecting you to. I have a question. How easy would it be to find the spyware on the source computer?"

"Hmmm... easier than tracking it from this end. Do you have a suspect already?"

"Maybe. How fast could you do it with direct access?"

"Not very. I'd still have to search the entire hard drive. Of course, if time is limited, I could probably reconfigure my search utility to run in the background and ping me when it completes the search. I can upload that in no time."

"Great. Can you have it ready by tomorrow morning?"

"Sure, as long as I'm paid overtime."

"Good. Call me when it's ready," I said, and hung up.

The fastest way to Neo was the Clark Street bus. I sat in a scantily cushioned seat, two green-haired college students entwined in each other's legs across from me and an elderly lady taking home her nightly groceries several seats ahead. I stared out at the host of lighted storefronts and apartment buildings as we cruised along, thinking about all the alderman had told me. If what he said was true, this investigation could take me to a very dicey place. I didn't particularly want to get tangled up in gang wars or factions of slave traders. That could get seriously messy. I had gotten used to a higher class of sleazebag since Frank took me on, and I hadn't dealt with true criminals since my days on the force. Have I mentioned that yet?

Right. The short of it is that I joined the Chicago Police Department right after college. I had always wanted to be a detective. After a couple of years on the beat, I passed the exams, and my dream came true. I was good too; I solved a lot of cases no one else could. Unfortunately, a lot of my collars didn't stick. My methods of investigation didn't jive with the district attorney's office. I had a habit of bending the rules a little too far—far enough so the perps slid off the rod of justice. Some said I crossed the line a few too many times and violated the rights of the offenders too often. I didn't see it that way though. I saw results.

And then one day a particularly heinous psychopath whom I had arrested was cut loose from a murder charge because I supposedly conducted an illegal search and seizure and coerced his confession. It was bullshit. The guy was guilty as sin. Later that week, he had the audacity to walk into a bar I frequented with a smug look on his face and make a snide comment about how I'd hit like a girl in the interrogation room. I snapped and beat the living snot out of him in front of all those witnesses: I broke his nose and three ribs, dislocated his elbow, and severely bruised his spleen before the other cops there could pull me off him. He spent two weeks in the hospital while I was brought up on charges of assault and battery. Needless to say, I lost my job.

After that, I fell into a pretty serious bout of depression and did a good bit of damage to my liver. At some point—I really have no idea how long I wallowed in self-pity—Frank found me and offered me a job. I owe a lot to that man. He never did tell me how he found me, but I think Larsen had something to do with it.

***

The bus driver called out the intersection I was waiting for, and I pulled the cord. I don't know why, but the ding signaling a stop is terribly satisfying.

I hopped off the bus and walked down the block toward the club.

As I got closer, I felt the *thump thump thump* of deep bass emanating from the building. Someone ahead of me opened the door, letting more of the rhythm and some of the melody escape into the night air.

It was a couple of minutes before ten. This place was reputed to be a late-night joint, so I hoped it wouldn't be too crowded and I could talk to the staff without interference.

Once inside, I realized interference from other people wouldn't be an issue. Being heard over the pulsating music, however, would be.

Just inside the door and to the right was the coat check, which I ignored. To the left was an elevated area with a bar made of concrete and topped with terrazzo marble. A long dance floor extended from there, lined on one wall with mirrors below cement archways. In the back, I could make out a DJ booth perched above a lounge area and opposite a stage for live bands. The whole place was lit with hues of purple and orange by Fresnel lights hanging from the ceiling. It gave me the sense that I was standing on Lower Wacker Drive looking out at the river—you know, if Satan had done the decorating.

I climbed up to the bar and waved at the bartender, who was busy cutting limes. He came over, then leaned over the bar and shouted in my ear, "What can I get you?"

"Information," I shouted back. "I'm looking for someone."

"Aren't we all." He smirked. "Most of the ladies don't get here until midnight. Have a drink and chill out till then."

I pulled out my wallet and flipped it open to my PI badge.

A lot of PI's don't carry a badge so that they don't run the risk of impersonating a police officer, which can end a career quickly. I like to have one, however, because it can open doors that would otherwise remain closed and locked. Some people who would clam up around a cop will talk to a private detective because they don't think we have any authority to arrest them for something they say—which is mostly true. I thought this might be one of those times. Drugs are pretty common in clubs, and I didn't want this guy to be afraid of me, but I did want him to take me seriously.

He glanced at it quickly and lost interest, but I held it out a little longer and waited until he took a closer look. His expression softened a little but remained wary.

Then I held up Ellie's Facebook photo on my cell phone. "Have you seen her lately?"

He squinted at the picture. "Couldn't say. Looks a little vanilla for this place. Talk to one of the wait staff. They see more faces than I do." With that, he went back to his limes.

I found a waitress pretty quickly—it wasn't really busy yet, so they were milling around aimlessly—and showed her the photo.

"Yeah, I think I've seen her in here a few times," the waitress chirped.

"Do you remember the last time she was in?"

"Not really. You should ask Eli. I think she hung out with him most of the time."

"Who's Eli?" She pointed to a corner of the bar where a guy sat in a plush booth.

"Thanks," I said, and headed in that direction.

Eli had spiky bleached-blond hair, perfectly applied eyeliner, and wore a black peacoat over a shirt that hugged his perfectly chiseled chest.

He gave me an appraising stare as I approached.

"Are you Eli?" I asked.

He didn't respond, just continued to stare.

"I'm told you're the man to see for the inside scoop on the ladies that come here." I hoped the compliment would break the ice.

He shrugged.

"Do you mind if I sit down?"

He shrugged again.

I pulled out the chair opposite him and sat.

"Nice jacket," I said.

"What do you want?" he tossed at me in a flippant, devil-may-care London accent.

"Okay, I'll skip the small talk. I'm looking for this girl," I showed him Ellie's picture. "I know she's been coming here and that you were seen with her on several occasions."

"Sure, I've seen her around. Hard to miss, actually. She's a fit bird. A bit too posh for this place, though."

His voice was deep and rich, with just a hint of tartness, kind of like a good barbecue sauce.

"When was the last time you saw her?"

"Couple of weeks ago, I think. Can't be sure. The nights all blend into each other at this point."

"Try a little harder." As far as I knew, this guy might have been the last person to talk to her before she disappeared. I needed him to tell me everything he could.

"Thinking makes me thirsty," he hinted.

I flagged down the waitress and ordered him another round.

"You said she was hard to miss. Why?"

"I have a thing for redheads. Something about a bonnie lass really gets me going," he flipped.

"What did you talk about?"

"Talk? We didn't. We danced. I hoped we would do more than that, but it turns out she was just a tease." His tone turned spiteful. "I don't like having my chain yanked, so I quit talking to the nit. No shortage of women here."

"Did she turn her attention to anyone else?"

"I don't bloody know. I don't pay attention to other blokes trying to get their knobs polished."

His attention began to wander. I could feel the hypnotic rhythm of the music pulling me into a trance as well.

"Come on, I'm sure you would've noticed if the tease left with another man," I plied.

"Maybe, but she didn't. She always left alone. That's how I know she was a tease."

By this point, I figured our conversation was over, so I paid his tab, left my card with him, and asked him to call if he could remember anything else. I doubted I'd hear from him, but you never know.

***

It was late, and I was beat. I didn't want to risk going back to the office in case it was being watched by whoever had tried to kill me. My place was still technically a crime scene, so I could-n't go back there. I decided to rent a room for the night and de-compress with an hour or two of mindless television before I crashed. Tomorrow was going to be a big day.

9

Ryley waited, somewhat impatiently, for his master to arrive. He had gotten the text a little before midnight and arrived at the specified location shortly after. It was almost two o'clock now.

At last, a figure stepped out from a steel-framed door into the alley. The darkness that hid his features was thicker than usual somehow—maybe due to the humidity from the recent rains. Ryley could smell the anger rolling off his Sire in waves. Something was up.

"Ryley!" his superior snapped.

Ryley didn't respond. The boss already knew exactly where he was; his senses were far better than Ryley's.

"Why is the detective still alive?"

"Harrison failed again," Ryley answered.

"Obviously, you idiot. But why?"

"He said it was pure chance, a one in a million coincidence. The detective ducked just as Harrison pulled the trigger."

"Fantastic. So tell him to try again."

Ryley hesitated. He didn't want to be the bearer of still more bad news. The resulting wrath could be the end of him, he knew. But this was his job, and he'd known all that it entailed when he signed up for it.

"There's a problem," he said once he worked up the nerve. "We've been cut off. Harrison is no longer on the job."

The boss's eyes narrowed to slits. "Is that so?" he hissed.

Expecting an onslaught of rage to descend upon him, Ryley closed his eyes and waited, but several heartbeats later, there was still only silence. He chanced a peek and realized his Sire was standing nose to nose with him. His ashen face filled Ryley's entire view. It was not contorted with anger, as he'd expected, but the placid expression it bore was far more terrifying. Ryley swallowed.

When his Sire spoke, it was almost a whisper. "Then we'll

deal with the bastard ourselves. Do it the old fashioned way: hunt him down and tear out his throat like the dog he is."

"Won't that draw attention?" Ryley chanced the question.

"Yes. Yes, it will."

10

Daylight peeked around the heavy drapes of my motel room window when I woke up. I rolled over and looked at the alarm clock on the nightstand. 10:04. Crap. I had overslept.

The night before, I had set my phone's alarm for eight o'-clock. I knew the battery was low, but I had hoped it would last the night. I leaned over the edge of the bed and fished it out of my pants pocket. Sure enough, the display was dark, and it didn't respond when I swiped the screen.

I rolled out of the bed, took a quick shower, and put my dirty clothes back on. This was the third day I had worn them, and they had developed a certain character.

I needed to make some phone calls, but my charger was in my apartment—which, as far as I knew, was still off limits. I'd need to make that phone call, too.

I went down to the lobby and paid for another night, bought a new charger from the Walgreens on the corner, and went back to the room and plugged in my phone.

The first call I made was to Alderman Juarez's office to set up an interview with his assistant, Jason Gallagher. The receptionist was much more accommodating this time. I made the appointment for two o'clock.

Next I called Mac. I think I woke him up; he sounded groggy when he picked up the line.

"Mac, tell me you have that program ready," I said a little too brusquely.

"Yeah, yeah," he grumbled. "What time is it?"

"Almost eleven," I replied. "Can you meet me at your shop at noon? We have an appointment at two to find out if your thing works."

"My thing works all right. I can give you several references if you want." A thousand comedians out of work, and Mac was trying to be funny.

"Ha ha. I'll see you in a few."

Next, I called Jack Larsen to find out where they were with the investigation. He told me they had identified the victim as Victor Sanz and had tracked down his address. His prints were in the system from prior arrests, but, as of yet, they had been unable to determine why he had been in my apartment or who could have killed him. The lead detective on the case, Rowe, hadn't had much luck. Jack warned me that Rowe wanted to question me again and that he was doing his best to keep him off my back. Unfortunately, they needed me to sign some papers before they could release the crime scene and let me back into my apartment. When I came in, Jack cautioned, I would probably have to sit down and talk to Mr. Rowe, so if I knew anything, it would be in my best interest to tell him now. I assured him that I didn't have any light to shed on the situation yet. I didn't have a reason to protect Juarez, but I also didn't want to complicate my own investigation at the moment.

When I got off the phone, it was time to head out. I debated leaving my phone in the room to fully charge, but decided to take it with me, just in case. I gave it ten minutes to build up what charge it could while I hit the head. Then I made my way to Mac's place.

Mac was dressed in khakis and a blue polo, with his black hair going crazy, looking every bit the quintessential computer nerd. He held up a flash drive when I walked in and told me he was ready.

"I'll need ten to fifteen minutes to upload the program and execute it to run in the background of the OS," he explained, "maybe a little longer if the system is password protected and I need to hack in."

"I can probably give you twenty minutes," I told him. "From what I remember, there's a conference room just off the hallway near the entrance. The assistant's office is farther down. The alderman is expecting us, so you shouldn't have any trouble getting in. I'll position myself so I can keep an eye on the hallway. When you're done, I'll see you leave and meet you outside."

"Sounds good," he said, sounding a little excited. It wasn't often he got to be surreptitious in his work. Then he added, "Did they find the guy who shot at you yesterday?"

"No, and I don't think they will."

"Should I be worried?" From the sound of it, he already was.

"Maybe. But I think if we stay around people, we'll be okay. Whoever's gunning for me doesn't want a lot of attention. Of that I'm sure."

"Okay, then."

Mac offered to drive, which I appreciated. We stopped off at a burrito place for lunch—I treated—then drove up Broadway to the ward office. Traffic was pretty busy, and we seemed to catch most of the lights red, so we arrived right at two.

Mac took a seat while I spoke to the receptionist. She greeted me with a smile, unlike the day before, then punched a button on the phone to inform Mr. Gallagher that his appointment was here. A few minutes later, he came out and shook my hand, then led me to the conference room. I took a seat facing the door, which forced Gallagher to sit across from me. So far, so good. He closed the door behind him, but thankfully there was a window through which I could watch for Mac. A minute or so later, I saw him walk down the hallway, following the receptionist. He flashed a goofy grin at me as he passed.

My plan was to have a very casual conversation with Mr. Gallagher, keeping him distracted and at ease the whole time. I doubted I'd get any helpful information out of him, especially if he had something to do with Ellie's kidnapping.

I asked him what he knew about Ellie's relationship with

the alderman.

"Arthur wants to marry her," he said warmly.

"Arthur?" From the way he said it, I assumed that was Juarez's first name, but it sounded awfully anglicized.

"Yes, sorry. His name is Arturo, but we've always called him Arthur."

Gallagher told me that he had known the alderman since college and he had always admired his ability to bring people together. "I knew he had one heck of a future in politics when he started a multicultural festival at school. He brought people with many different backgrounds together to celebrate both their uniqueness and commonalities. That first gala was like a dream. I'd never seen anything like it before. But it didn't stop there. He kept reaching out to the students, forging friendships and bonds that had never existed before. He's been able to carry that ability into his role as alderman and it's been invaluable. We called it 'mutually respectful diversity' during his campaign."

He went on to describe the depth of Arthur's feelings for Ellie and his desire to take their relationship to the next level. It was on Jason's advice that he had kept it a secret until the right time arose to announce their engagement. Jason expressed some regret at this fact; she might not have gone missing if they had announced it sooner.

Jason wasn't aware of Ellie's visits to Neo or of any other recent pursuits, but the visit didn't surprise him, given her strong desire to experience new things and immerse herself in the city. That was one of the things that attracted Arthur to her. They had met at a street festival, after all, one of many in which Chicagoans come together to celebrate their heritage with food, drink, and music.

The way Jason told it, theirs was a storybook romance, and both of them had been swept away by the affair—at least, at first. Then reality had settled in, and the longer they dated, the trickier the politics got. But their love seemed to be real, and they were sticking it out and dealing with the issues the secrecy caused. And then she had disappeared.

Gallagher was extremely forthcoming and didn't seem to be holding anything back. It was one of the easiest interviews I've ever held. Either he honestly wanted to help his friend, or he was involved up to his beaky little nose and was trying his best to appear otherwise.

After about twenty minutes, I saw Mac walk past the door again. He looked a little nervous but gave me a thumbs up anyway. I probably could have kept Gallagher talking for another twenty minutes, but I decided to wrap it up and see what Mac had to say.

I thanked Jason for his candor and assured him that he had been a big help, then excused myself from the conference room.

I smiled at the receptionist as I left and found Mac waiting for me outside as planned.

"What's got you rattled?" I asked quickly.

"Nothing big. Nobody knew the admin password, so I had to hack it. I was worried about how long it was taking me."

"Well, Gallagher was a talker, so no worries. I didn't even have to get creative. How long before we find something out?"

Mac sighed in relief.

"A couple of hours probably. Depends on how many files are on his hard drive." We started walking back to his Beetle. "So what next?"

"Huh? Well, I have another... um... interview." I hesitated. "If you want to give me a lift, I'd appreciate it, but other than that, I don't think you should get involved."

"An interview, huh?" Mac crinkled his bushy black eyebrows. "I take it you don't think that guy will be as friendly as the last."

"Probably not. Best you don't stick around for it."

***

The address I had was in Rogers Park, the northernmost neighborhood within the city limits. Like most areas of the city, it had a good side and a not-so-good-side. We were headed for the latter. Most of the residential streets had those little traffic circles that are supposed to prevent drive-by shootings. There was plenty of low-income housing, gang activity, and drug trade, but I'd seen plenty of that during my days on the force. Knowing that I'd be dealing with an informant I'd never met and whose face I'd never seen meant I'd need a little cash to help grease the wheels, so I had Mac stop at an ATM. I'd also probably be talking to some locals, so I needed to adopt a grittier persona.

I held my eyelids open, resisting the urge to blink. When Mac politely asked what the hell I was doing, I explained that I was trying to make my eyes appear bloodshot. Then I pinched my cheeks a few times to get them nice and rosy.

As we neared the address, I had Mac slow down so I could get a feel for the layout of the buildings—and find a couple of quick routes to a busy street where I could catch a cab in case I needed to beat a hasty retreat.

Ahead of us on the right, outside a large brick apartment building surrounded by a security fence, loitered three black kids. I say kids, though they could have been in their early twenties. Their attire was fairly typical urban fashion: skinny jeans and hoodies. One wore a puffy winter coat; two of them wore tan colored work boots, while one had on bright purple sneakers. As we cruised by, I saw that this building was the place I was looking for. I didn't like it. Those guys could be lookouts... or they could just be kids hanging out on the corner after school. Only one way to find out.

I had Mac drop me off on the next block up, around the corner. He asked if I wanted him to wait, but I assured him that would be unnecessary. While I hoped I could take care of this quickly, it might take a while just to find the guy.

Once the car had turned down the next street, I rounded the corner and pulled out a cigarette, lit it, and let it dangle from my lips. I let myself look nervous: eyes darting, constantly looking behind me. The three kids eyed me as I approached and stifled their laughter. I stopped just out of arm's reach, shifted my weight from foot to foot, and fiddled with my own hat.

One of them finally spoke up. "Whatchu want?"

I cleared my throat. "I'm looking for Jimmy."

"Yeah," the one wearing the purple sneakers said, "what you want Jimmy for?"

I cleared my throat again and glanced around nervously.

"Business," I coughed.

They looked askance at each other.

The first one spoke again, "Jimmy ain't got no bizness wit you... pig."

"I ain't no cop," I told him.

They glanced at each other again. The third one, the quiet one, looked a little less comfortable than the other two.

"Whatever," Sneakers said. They turned from me and started to walk away.

I stepped forward and grabbed the one in the puffy coat by the sleeve. He whirled around and swung at me with his other arm. I bobbed my head out of the way and caught his wrist with my free hand. When I did, my jacket must have come open, revealing the pistol at my side. The kid's eyes went wide.

"I just need to see Jimmy. He's got something I need." I tried to make my voice sound strained, desperate.

The kid looked over his shoulder to the quiet one and shouted, "Get outta here, Jim! Dude's got a gun!"

The two other boys took off in opposite directions. Sneakers went west across the street, while the one I presumed to be

Jimmy went east along the sidewalk. I shoved Puffy Coat aside and went after Jimmy.

I hate running. I mean, I really despise it. I don't like the way it feels when my feet repeatedly slam into concrete, jarring the bones all the way to my inner ear. It's not that I'm bad at running—I do cardio on a regular basis, and I'm capable of pretty fast bursts of speed. I don't even lose my breath, which is pretty strange, given my taste for Camels. I just simply don't like to run.

Jimmy saw me coming after him and kicked it into high gear, heading for the gate to the courtyard of the complex. He took a hard left, slammed the gate open—apparently the lock was broken—and tore across the courtyard with me in hot pursuit. Instead of heading for the main door, he angled toward the side of the building. Given the layout of the place, I figured there was a side entrance or maintenance access over there.

I was gaining on him—his clodhoppers were slowing him down—but if he made it inside the building, I would lose the advantage.

He rounded the corner about three seconds before I did. To my surprise, he had disappeared from view. I didn't see any doors, but a fraction of a second later I realized there was a gap in the wall, a small alley of sorts. I skidded to a halt, thinking this would be the perfect spot for an ambush, then poked my head around the corner. Jimmy was about fifty feet down the alley, trying to jimmy open a door. Pun intended. The far end of the alley was walled off to present a solid facade to the facing street; apparently the complex was two separate buildings, with this alley offering rear access to both units.

I double-timed it toward Jimmy. He looked up, saw me coming, and put his shoulder into the door. It burst open just as I got there. He tumbled inside, then scrambled to his feet. I launched myself at him and hit him at the waist with a solid tackle, and we both went to the floor. I expected him to put up a fight, but he just lay there groaning softly.

I picked myself up off the floor and gently rolled the boy over. He was breathing, but unconscious. Even in the dim light, I could see a knot forming on his forehead. He must have bonked his noggin pretty good on the cement floor when I tackled him. Great. I still needed to talk to him, so it looked like I'd have to stick around for a while until he woke up.

I took in my surroundings. We were in a dingy hallway that had never been painted, the gray concrete walls turning black in spots from accumulated dirt and grime. It smelled of mildew and cat piss. Several doors lined the hallway, so I went to investigate them. I didn't think Jimmy would be running away again anytime soon.

The first door was a maintenance closet holding shelves of industrial style cleaner, a few HVAC supplies, and a mop that looked so crunchy I imagined it would disintegrate if someone tried to use it. The second door led to a boiler room. It was dark; I had to search around the wall for a few minutes before I found the light switch. The single, naked bulb brightened the place just enough that I could see. The boiler hadn't been lit yet for the year, so I decided this room would be the perfect place to wait with Sleeping Beauty, even if it was pretty grungy.

I went back to the hallway, picked Jimmy up under the shoulders, and dragged him into the boiler room. After propping him up against the wall I returned to the janitor's closet and grabbed a roll of duct tape that had seen better days and the bucket the mop was standing in. I flipped the bucket upside down for a stool, then taped Jimmy's hands and ankles together. After that, I searched him; I didn't want to get stuck with a knife or something because I wasn't thorough.

His wallet was mostly empty, save for a five dollar bill and his driver's license, which confirmed that this was, in fact, Jimmy Armstrong. The kid was barely eighteen. I put the wallet back in his pants and searched his hoodie. Here I came up with a dime bag of MJ, a pipe, and a teener of ice, which I set on the floor in front of me. Then I lit another cigarette, sat on the bucket, and waited for him to wake up.

11

Jimmy groaned. His eyes fluttered open. Then he saw me sitting on the bucket in front of him and let out a string of expletives that would have impressed any sailor. When he stopped to take a breath, I interrupted.

"Are you finished? You've been out for an hour, and I have places to be. I'd like to get down to business."

He told me I could go and have intimate relations with myself, only more succinctly and with less imagination.

I grunted, then continued, nonplussed. "Here's the deal. I have several of your possessions, which likely hold some value." I indicated the paraphernalia lying on the floor. "I believe you have some information which would be valuable to me. If you answer my questions, nothing happens to your stuff and I'll give you $60. If, however, you continue to be an ass, it will all go bye-bye."

"Whatever, man. Why didn't you text me? Didn't they tell you how this works down at the station?"

"I already told you, I'm not a cop."

"Who do you work for, then?"

I flashed him a smile. "Now, now. You're the one that has to answer the questions. So, who would I need to talk to if I wanted to buy a girl?"

"You knocked me out and tied me up so you could find out where to get a hooker?" he asked incredulously. "Try Craigslist, dude."

I picked up his baggie of weed. "I'm not talking about hookers, you moron. I'm talking about something more permanent."

He stared at me blankly. "Huh?

"A slave, you idiot. Who would I talk to about buying a slave?"

"A slave?" he repeated slowly. "Man, I don't know nothing about that."

"That's not what my sources say." I dumped the bag of marijuana on the floor.

"Whoa, whoa! Dude!" he hollered. "Not cool!"

"I hear you have an inside track on the human trafficking market in this city. What do you know?

"Aw, man, come on. That's above my pay grade."

Next, I picked up the baggie of meth.

"Hey, wait a minute," he pleaded.

"Spill it, or I will."

"Look, look," he stammered. "I don't know much, but I've heard some rumors."

I put the baggie back on the ground.

"I don't know nothin' about buying anybody, but word is if you need some quick cash, there's people offering a finder's fee for homeless kids, people that fall through the cracks... you know, people no one will miss."

"Now we're getting somewhere," I told him. "How do you contact them?"

He looked sheepish, then said in a quiet voice, "Craigslist."

I picked up the meth again.

"I'm being straight with you, man. They say you have to go on there and post something about dreadlocks in the beauty section. They'll contact you and ask if you can dye them red or something. Then you reply with the location of the homeless guy. That's all I know, I swear."

"See now, that wasn't so hard, was it?" I pulled out my notepad and wrote down *red dreadlocks, Craigslist, homeless people*. Then I laid three twenty-dollar bills on the floor and said, "I'm going to free your hands now. Don't do anything stupid. Hopefully, we won't see each other again." I stripped the duct tape off his wrists; he remained calm. After that, I saw myself out of the boiler room and into the courtyard while Jimmy was un-doing his feet.

We had been inside longer than I thought; it had gotten dark. Autumn was in full swing, and the days kept getting short-er. I didn't relish the idea of hanging out in this neighborhood any longer than necessary, so I hustled toward a busier street to hail a cab.

I made it a block before all hell broke loose.

The side streets were deserted and I was heading for an alley I knew cut through to Clark Street rather than walk around the block. I must have felt a change in air pressure or heard a muted footfall, because I sensed someone behind me. I was step-ping to the right, intending to pivot on my right foot to face the newcomer, when I took a hard hit on the left shoulder. Some-thing popped.

If I hadn't taken that step, I would have been hit square in the back and knocked face first to the pavement. As it was, the force of the blow spun me around and knocked me off balance and onto my back.

Another body hit the ground beyond me. Apparently my attacker had gone for a full body tackle, and his momentum had toppled him over as well.

I rolled over and pushed myself to my knees, expecting to see Jimmy or one of his posse. Instead, a guy in a black leather biker jacket, purple hair, and several facial piercings was already back on his feet and coming at me fast. Too fast.

Before I could get to my feet, the guy picked me up by the front of my jacket and hurled me into the wall of the alley. I flew a good five feet through the air, then hit the bricks and lost my breath.

I couldn't believe this guy was that strong. He wasn't big, just wiry. I didn't have long to think about it, though, because he was on me in a heartbeat. He grabbed me by the shirt and slammed my back into the wall again. No one had ever gotten the drop on me like this.

He pinned me to the wall with his left hand and cocked his right arm back, aiming a punch at my face. I took the opportunity to grab the ring in his lower lip and jerked down as hard as I could, feeling it tear through flesh.

The punk screamed and grabbed his lip with both hands, giving me half a second's reprieve. I kicked out as hard as I could at his left kneecap and felt a sickening crunch on impact. He howled in pain as his leg crumpled beneath his own weight. I moved away from the wall and tried to step around him.

The guy must have been high as a kite, because he jumped up, supporting himself on his good leg and letting the other hang limp. He grabbed my wrist and spun me face-first into the wall. My vision tunneled, and the metallic taste of blood filled my mouth. A fist hammered into my side, and I swore I heard a rib crack. I sank to the ground.

The maniac handled me like a rag doll. He grabbed me under the armpits, lifting me back to my feet, and flipped me around so I could see his face. The next thing I knew, his fingers were wrapped around my throat, and his clawlike nails dug into my skin. I swear to God, this tweaker picked my two-hundred-twenty-pound frame a good six inches off the pavement.

I panicked.

My left arm still wasn't responding, so I tried to pry his fingers away with one hand, but his grip was like a vise clamped around my windpipe.

"Struggle all you want, kitten," the psycho hissed. "You've used up all your lives, and curiosity is about to kill you."

I couldn't speak, and darkness was crowding in around the edges of my vision. I knew I didn't have long, so I dropped my hand and reached into my open jacket, feeling for the grip of my pistol.

He opened his mouth, revealing a maw full of pointy teeth. Great. Not only was this guy hyped up on some crazy strength-boosting drug, but he was one of those vampire wannabes that filed his teeth. This just kept getting better.

He pulled me closer and sank his fangs into the side of my neck.

Just then my fingers closed around the textured grip of the .380. My thumb found the safety, and I clicked it off as I yanked it from the holster.

I pulled the trigger; a loud crack filled the air.

The pressure on my neck eased as the freak dropped me. He staggered back a couple of steps, clutching his stomach. He looked down at the wound, then back at me. His face twisted in rage, and he snarled something incoherent.

I pulled the trigger again, aiming for center mass.

Impossibly, he took a step forward. I fired two more rounds in rapid succession. This time, the force knocked him backward on his ass. He sat there for half a second, then toppled over in a heap.

I didn't wait to see what else would happen. I shoved the pistol back in its holster and dragged myself to my feet, then clamped a hand around my neck, applying pressure to staunch the flow of blood running over my shoulder.

The ground pitched beneath my feet as I staggered through the alley toward the main street. I glanced over my shoulder and saw the man begin to stir. How was he still alive?

I stumbled over a trash can and nearly fell to the asphalt. Pain had replaced the adrenaline that had coursed through my body: my nose throbbed, my ribs were screaming, and my neck was on fire. I knew it was only a matter of time before I passed out. Now I wished I *had* asked Mac to stick around.

I burst out of the alley. The sound of traffic assaulted my pulsating head. Headlights blinded me, and I tripped over the curb. Brakes squealed to a halt in front of me. To my utter relief, it was a cab. I vaguely remember pouring myself into the back-seat and telling the cabbie to take me to a hospital over loud accusations of trying to get myself killed. Then I sank into blissful blackness.

12

The respite didn't last for long. Fractured images of fanged monsters lurking in the darkness swam through my dreams, shattering and reforming like a macabre stained-glass kaleidoscope.

Then I was gliding soundlessly above downtown Chicago like in the establishing shot of some summer blockbuster. I saw in an otherworldly spectrum, not the twinkling whites and yellows of artificial lighting that suffuse an urban landscape, but writhing ribbons and knots of blue and red energy. They seemed somehow significant, but their meaning eluded me.

The vision faded, and was replaced with my own grizzled image floating before me. I reached out and touched the smooth surface of a mirror. For a moment, all I could see in the reflection was my bruised and battered face, but soon ghostly impressions of buildings materialized behind me. I glanced over my shoulder and saw only darkness, but the silhouettes in the mirror remained. There was no color to them, just mottled shades of gray that shifted and shimmered. I reached out again, and this time the surface of the mirror gave way, rippling beneath my touch. The shadowy figures walking the streets behind my reflection paused and turned featureless faces toward me.

Something about this disturbed me, stirred my consciousness. I began to hear muffled voices. The darkness around me lightened, and the mirror shattered.

I woke up in the hospital, with a heart monitor beeping rhythmically by my shoulder. Everything hurt. My face felt swollen, and only a trickle of air wheezed through my nose.

I opened my eyes a skosh, wincing as the harsh light bombarded my eyelids. Something tugged at my wrist, and I slid my gaze up the IV tubing to the stand where a heavyset nurse was adjusting the bag. She hadn't noticed I was awake yet. I debated getting her attention. On one hand, she seemed preoccupied, and I didn't feel like talking. On the other, I hurt like hell and thought I might score some painkillers.

"Ow," I grunted hoarsely. It was all I could muster at the moment.

"Good morning, sunshine," she said. Great. She was going to be all perky. "My name's Enid. I'll be your nurse today until six o'clock. If you need anything, just let me know. All right, sugar?"

"Ow," I said again.

She told me she'd get me some Percocet to take the edge off my pain and indicated that I had a visitor. I flicked my eyes in the direction she gestured and saw Frank slumped in a chair in the corner, eyes closed, chin resting on his chest. Enid stepped over and put her hand on his shoulder. He looked up at her and then at me before righting himself. Then Enid hustled out of the room, hopefully to get some meds.

Frank yawned, rubbed his eyes, stretched his arms, and shifted his weight forward, giving me the once-over.

"You look like hell," he said.

The outpouring of affection nearly brought me to tears.

"You too," I croaked.

He laughed at that, then turned serious.

"We've got some things to talk about, I think. But before we do, you'll have to answer a few questions from someone else. There's a detective just outside. He wanted to wake you as soon as he arrived, but I wouldn't let him."

As if on cue, Detective Rowe stepped through the door, saying something to somebody over his shoulder. He looked irritated as all get out. He shot daggers at Frank, who simply leaned back in the chair. His glare settled on me, taking in the extent of my injuries, I supposed, and he grunted.

"You've been busy," he snapped. "What were you doing in Roger's Park?"

"Working," I told him.

"Care to expound on that?"

"I was following a lead on a missing person case."

"Why don't you tell me what happened that led to this?" He waved a hand at my injuries.

"I finished my interview and was walking along the street to catch a cab, and some guy came at me from out of nowhere."

"Do you know who he was?"

"No."

"Is he connected to your case?"

"I dunno. He didn't give me a chance to ask." The detective's tone rubbed me the wrong way; I couldn't keep the snark at bay. His eye twitched, and his jaw clenched.

"What did you do then?"

I paused for a second before responding. "I defended myself."

He snorted, "Defended yourself? You told the ER medics you shot someone, and there are four rounds missing from the magazine of your sidearm. That's a little excessive, don't you think?"

I didn't remember saying anything to the doctors or nurses, but then again, I didn't remember anything after passing out in the cab.

"No," I answered. "He tried to bash my skull in and rip my throat out with his teeth. The first shot didn't stop him, so I put in three more rounds before he finally dropped."

"He took three bullets at point blank range and didn't go down?" Rowe's voice brimmed with incredulity.

"No one's more surprised than me. I think he was high or something."

Rowe paused. I guess he was trying to figure out what concoction of pharmaceuticals could give someone that kind of resilience.

"I've read your file, Gray. You have a history of gratuitous violence. How do I know you didn't pick this fight?"

Frank shifted uncomfortably in his seat.

"That was different," I muttered. I couldn't blame Rowe for going down this road—I'd be thinking the same thing myself if I was in his position—but I had to derail it.

"How so?"

"Look at me. I didn't do this to myself. I was blindsided. The guy was trying to kill me, and he almost succeeded. Look at the body if you don't believe me. I never touched him... until, you know, I shot him." Ack. Eloquence was eluding me. "But that was a last resort."

"Perhaps. There's one problem with that—we can't find the body."

I shot a look at Frank, who shrugged.

"What do you mean?"

"After the call came in from the hospital, we searched a four block radius around where the cab picked you up. We found some blood stains on the sidewalk, but no body, not even a blood trail leading away from the scene."

"I... huh... that's weird." I didn't know what else to say.

Detective Rowe sighed deeply and pinched the bridge of his nose.

"Look, Gray, I want to believe you. I really do." What was it with this guy? He had to know I didn't believe his nice guy act. "But I know you're not telling me everything. I don't know what, exactly, but this entire business is riddled with holes. Between the dead guy in your apartment, an apparent shooting at your place of business, and now this... it's no coincidence. And when I connect the dots, which I will, if you're behind any of it, it won't go well for you.

"I wish I could be of more help." It was only a little lie.

"Right," he sniffed. "Fortunately for you, without more evidence to corroborate or refute your story, and without an actual body, I can't arrest you. Rest assured, however, that I will be watching you very closely. If you do happen to *remember* anything else, your cooperation will be noted."

He shot another look at Frank, then walked out of the room.

Frank got up and followed him to the door. When he was satisfied that the detective wasn't lingering outside to eavesdrop, he returned to his chair and said, "All right, Gray, tell me what's going on."

I told him everything: the discovery of Victor Sanz' corpse, his connection with the alderman, my suspicions that the attempts on my life were, in fact, related, and that it was all somehow connected to Ellie McCarthy. I knew I could trust Frank. I also knew that, besides withholding evidence from the police, I was guilty of nothing. Frank remained quiet while I spoke, though his eyebrows rose on several occasions, and when I told him about the possibility of human traffickers and the info I'd gotten from Jimmy, they just about crawled off his face.

When I finished spilling the beans, we both sat in silence for a few moments, and then he let out a low whistle.

"Damn, Gray, what have you gotten yourself into? This is dangerous territory. I think you might be in over your head. Let me make some phone calls and see what I can dig up."

"No," I said. "Whoever's behind Ellie's kidnapping is dangerous. I've already got a target on my back, and I don't want you getting involved. You've got family to worry about. I don't. Stay out of it."

Frank looked as if he was about to argue but thought better of it. I certainly hoped he'd listen. He had a wife and two kids. Back when he first hired me, they would invite me over for dinner. I know I wasn't good company at the time, but his wife, Nancy, took my intrusion on their private life in stride and always welcomed me with a hug and a home-cooked meal. I don't think I'd have gotten back on my feet like I did without her motherly influence. I wanted them as far away from this situation as possible.

Frank told me that Mac had left a message at the office—he had some information for me, but my cell kept going straight to voice-mail. It was probably dead again, since I'd barely charged it before leaving the motel. I asked Frank to give Mac a call and let him know where I was and that he could swing by the hospital if he had time. It didn't look like I'd be going anywhere for a while.

***

The rest of the day passed uneventfully. Frank left before lunch, and I napped off and on once the meds had eased the pain into a dull ache.

At the shift change, the new nurse introduced herself, a short blonde girl named Tiffany with a cute little snub nose. She pretty much left me alone after that. I turned on the TV and surfed around until I found reruns of "I Love Lucy." I've never been a big fan of the show, but I found myself mildly entertained. I made it through three or four episodes before I fell asleep.

The next time I woke up, everything was dark except for what soft light spilled through the doorway from the hall. I was immediately aware of another presence in the room. It took a few moments for my eyes to adjust to the dim ambient light, but once they did, I spotted the figure seated in the same chair Frank had been in earlier, a shadow among shadows.

I tensed, expecting another attack, and my muscles screamed in protest. I was in no condition to fight, and lying in bed was a terrible position from which to mount a defense. I was completely vulnerable, and I didn't like it one bit.

"Relax, Mr. Gray," came a silky voice from the corner. "I'm not here to hurt you."

"Who are you?" I asked, not relaxing in the slightest.

The figure leaned forward in the chair so that what little light came through the door fell on his face. He was a handsome man with high cheekbones and a square jaw that bore a heavy five o'clock shadow. Strands of tousled brown hair fell over a pronounced forehead, giving him an unkempt and disarming appearance. Most people, I imagine, never looked beyond that initial impression. If they did, they would see what I saw: that it was a carefully crafted façade. His eyes told the true story. A sharp hazel flecked with gold, they focused intensely on me, watching every movement, every breath. Measuring. Assessing. They were the eyes of a hunter, one that carefully stalks his prey, hidden in plain sight, seeks out every strength and weakness, calculates the perfect method of attack, strikes with absolute precision, and almost never fails. This was a very dangerous man.

"My name," he said, "is Fletcher A. Harrison, the third."

13

"What do you want?" I asked carefully.

"To meet the one that got away." Harrison's tone was light, curious.

"What's that supposed to mean?"

"You have survived three attempts on your life in as many days. Considering the nature of those who want you dead, that is a significant achievement."

"And what, exactly, do you know about those people?" I asked, not sure I wanted to hear the answer.

"Less than I would like, but more than I can tell you."

That was a stupid non-answer. But you can learn a lot about someone by what they won't say. I didn't like what my gut was telling me about this guy. Time to see what else he wouldn't tell me.

"I used to do a lot of fishing, you know. My old man would take me out on the lake in this little jon boat. Way too small of a boat for such a big piece of water, if you ask me, but he liked it. We'd go out for hours on the weekend, drowning one worm after another. We caught some fish, but we lost a lot too. At night, he'd go down to the bar and tell stories about the ones that got away. You know what I learned from that?"

He said nothing, but he quirked up the corner of an eye-brow, so I continued.

"I learned that nobody really cares about the one that got away except the guy who lost him."

At this, the corner of his mouth twitched up a bit. Ah, mi-croexpressions. And... damn, this wasn't good news.

"So are you here to finish the job? Should be like shooting fish in a barrel." I figured if I was about to die, I might as well get in one more good pun.

The shadowy figure cracked a smile and chuckled.

"You are quite safe from me. I don't fish for pleasure," he said, continuing the metaphor.

Okay, so now I knew I had a contract killer staring at me—most likely the one who had killed Victor Sanz and shot at me behind the office. But if he said I was safe from him, that meant he wasn't on the job anymore.

"What changed?" I asked.

He shrugged. "Politics, I suppose."

"What's to keep me from pushing this button and calling security on you?"

He smirked. "On what grounds? A conversation about fishing?"

He had a point. Besides, if I could keep him talking, I might learn enough to figure out my next move.

"Am I still in danger?"

"Most assuredly. The rules of the game are changing. What once played out in the shadows is moving into the light. You have seen things that shouldn't be seen, things that cannot be unseen. Pieces are moving in unorthodox ways. And you, Mr. Gray are caught in the middle."

Ugh, more conspiracy theories and cloak-and-dagger crap. I must have rolled my eyes, because Harrison adopted a sour expression.

"I am a small piece on the board," he said, more seriously. "There are many others. And while I am no longer in play, you are still a threat, I think."

"To whom?"

He didn't answer.

"Great. So basically you're telling me 'congratulations for being alive, watch your ass.'"

He leaned back in the chair again.

"It's not your ass that I would be concerned about, given your last encounter."

I was suddenly very aware of the burning sensation in my neck. My hand instinctively went to the wound. So the freak who attacked me was connected to the McCarthy case. I figured as much, but Harrison's remark seemed to confirm it. As mysterious as this Fletcher Harrison was, and despite his penchant for speaking in riddles and metaphors, at least I had gathered a few more pieces to the puzzle. Now I just needed to fit them all together.

"So what's next? You going to tell me to back off with my investigation if I want to stay alive? 'Cause that's not going to happen. I'm as stubborn as they come, and now I've got a bone to pick."

"Not at all. You're free to do whatever you want, though I'm not sure backing off now would keep you alive. If you wish to survive, you need to be prepared for what you'll find. There is a very dark world through the looking glass, and once you step through, there is no going back. Unlike the Jabberwock, the monsters that reside there do not vanish simply because you stop believing in them."

Goose flesh prickled up my arm, and a shiver shuddered through my spine. I didn't like this conversation at all.

"Why tell me any of this? Why are you really here?" Harrison had a dog in this race somewhere, and if I could ferret it out, it might give me the upper hand down the road.

He took a deep breath and exhaled slowly through his nose. "I want you to succeed. My motives for that are... complicated."

"Stop talking in riddles, then, and give me some real answers."

He flashed a tight smile. "I have certain obligations that I dare not violate. Information is a dangerous weapon, and I am bound by non-disclosure agreements, so I apologize for not being more direct."

"All right, then. What *can* you tell me about the people I'm up against?"

There was a moment's silence while he considered the question.

Then, "Are you familiar with lateral thinking puzzles, Mr. Gray?"

"You mean like five-minute mysteries?" I was pretty good at figuring them out. My old man used to try to stump me with them when I was in high school.

"Yes. What is the key to solving them?"

"Questioning your assumptions. There's always something in the setup that leads you to a false assumption that's so basic you don't realize you've made it."

"Precisely," he purred. "For example, if I told you that Fred and Betty were lying dead on the floor in a puddle of water with broken glass around them, what false assumptions would you need to dispel before figuring out what happened?" This was one of the first five minute mysteries I'd ever heard. I knew exactly where he was going with this.

"That Fred and Betty are people. The setup doesn't say it explicitly, but most people assume it's the case. Once you figure out that Fred and Betty are fish, the answer is obvious."

"Very good. I would suggest, Mr. Gray, that you approach this case as you would one of those puzzles. Impossibility is often an illusion created by our own beliefs."

I mulled that over for a moment.

Harrison got to his feet and, with the barest whisper of movement, came to stand beside the hospital bed. "Are you a reader, Mr. Gray? I am, and I find so much can be learned that way. So many... connections can be made. Do your homework. A storm is coming, but every dark cloud has a silver lining. Good luck." With that, he turned and walked out the door, leaving me with a hundred more questions.

I couldn't go back to sleep after the assassin left. In the darkness, I played the words of our conversation again and again in my head. Of all the interviews I've ever done, this one was the most puzzling. Though he had spoken only in vague terms and had not once given me any specifics, I felt like he had verified several of my suspicions and firmed up a lead. But there was something else to what he said, something I was missing. I couldn't put my finger on it yet, but I got the feeling he had told me more than I realized.

I let the words tumble through my brain again. Shadows moving into light. Things that shouldn't be seen. Monsters through the looking glass. False assumptions. Dark clouds with silver linings. Do your homework.

I knew what the last one meant: I needed to do more research. I was now fairly certain that this group of human traffickers was behind Ellie's disappearance and that all the attempts on my life were meant to keep things under wraps. It didn't bode well that the police weren't on top of this either. That meant that the group had connections to the authorities, either in the PD or higher up. My priority was to find Ellie, but to do that, I needed to know more about this group. What was their market? Would she be overseas by now, or did they keep things local?

Harrison had also told me that my life would never be the same after this case. I'd seen a lot of ugliness in the city, but this sounded like corruption so evil it would change the way I viewed the world forever. If that was true, I needed to know what I was getting into before I took the plunge. Not that knowing would stop me, but you can only improvise your way out of bad situations for so long before they catch up with you. I wanted to be as prepared as possible. Unfortunately, I couldn't do anything stuck in a hospital bed. I had half a mind to pull out the IVs and make good my escape, but just the thought of standing up hurt. If I was going to be of any use, I needed to heal.

14

The raised voices through the door were nothing new. Brenda had heard many arguments since she began working here six months ago. How her world had changed in just six short months. This job had seemed like a gift from God: fifteen dollars an hour as receptionist and office assistant in a boutique real estate company. She could pay her rent on time every month and even afford the childcare provider the company recommended. The pay didn't go much beyond that, but it was way better than she was used to.

The honeymoon period lasted less than two months. In that time, she had learned that the company she worked for dealt very little in residential real estate, as their storefront suggested. Their primary business was warehousing, storage, and miscellaneous real-estate holdings. She quickly figured out that the business was involved in a number of shady dealings. She would've quit, gone to the police, and reported the activity, but before she'd worked up the nerve, the boss had called her into his office. It was the first time she'd spoken with him directly. All her prior dealings had been with the office manager, a middle-aged woman with a worn-down, defeated air about her.

The boss scared her. Something about him unnerved her completely, set her teeth on edge. He was tall and thick-necked, with a deep voice but a callous tone. His beady eyes glared out from beneath bushy black eyebrows. She got the impression that he had spent time in prison.

When he called her into his office, she started sweating immediately—a very unladylike response, but she couldn't help it. The nameplate next to his door read Mr. Brown. She timidly sat down in the folding metal chair in front of his desk, and he proceeded to inform her that the real estate business was more complicated than it appeared on the surface. He didn't expect her to understand all the nuances, but he did expect her to be mindful of her place in the company. She might hear and see things that she didn't understand, but it was totally normal, nothing untoward. He then commented on how small and fragile her son was, only two years old, and what a tragedy it would be for him if she made any rash decisions and lost her job, her income, her... security.

The threat was thinly veiled, but she knew immediately that there was more to it than just losing her job. Several days later, she started receiving anonymous emails containing pictures of her son at the daycare. They were obviously taken from outside the building, looking in. There were no notes or words attached— just the photos—but the message was clear. We're watching.

Brenda soon noticed that the same man followed her to and from work: not too close to draw attention, but close enough that he was always in her line of sight. And so her dream job became a nightmare, a curse from the Devil himself. She was trapped, fearing for her son's life, and so she did what she had to do. She showed up on time, kept her mouth shut, answered the phone politely, and tried to ignore anything she heard.

This evening, however, the yelling was especially difficult to ignore. The boss's resonant baritone echoed down the hall from the office, where he was speaking with some young British guy she'd seen a handful of times but had never been introduced to.

"You've got to get rid of her! She's a liability! We shouldn't take that risk!"

Brenda had no idea who they were talking about, but it had her attention.

There was a second's pause, then a loud thud. The office walls shook; something clattered to the floor inside.

"Never..." started the British fellow, but then his volume slid too low to hear. "You forget... Mine!... Don't care..." The words were an audible punctuation, but without the rest, Brenda couldn't make heads or tails of the conversation.

85

After a moment, the boss's door flung open and slammed into the wall. He walked out, red-faced, boiling with rage.

Brenda strained to keep her eyes glued to the monitor in front of her. The time on the screen showed 5:45. Outside, dusk would be gathering. Only fifteen minutes before she could leave. She tried to melt into her chair, hoping not to be noticed.

It didn't work. He stopped right beside her, across the divider. She could feel his glare boring into her, daring her to acknowledge his presence. It took every ounce of her control not to react, not to shrink from him, to pretend that she'd heard nothing.

Then she was saved when the other man slid through the office door and glided down the hallway. He was a good-looking guy. A solid black, slim Armani suit hugged his trim figure, contrasting with his shock of blonde hair.

The boss looked up, huffed, and stormed out the front door.

"Sorry about that, Duck," came a rich English accent. "Had a bit of a scuff in there. Nothing to worry yourself about." The man flashed a toothy smile at her. Relief washed over Brenda. She smiled hesitantly back at him. Perhaps things weren't as bleak as they seemed. This man must be upper management, or something, to have such authority over Mr. Brown. Perhaps she could share her concerns with him.

The Brit pushed lightly off the counter and started for the exit. Without looking back, he said, "Give that boy of yours a squeeze for me."

Terror seized her, immediately erasing her moment of comfort; her stomach twisted into knots.

15

Breakfast at the hospital was awful, and the coffee was worse. I'd hoped to be discharged today, but I hadn't seen a doctor yet.

My bladder had been pestering me about needing to be emptied. I was debating whether to get out of bed to use the john or call the nurse for a bedpan when Mac stopped by with a giant coffee from Dunkin' Donuts. I told my bladder to put a cork in it; coffee had the floor for the moment.

"Bless you," I said as he handed me the piping hot Styrofoam cup.

He nodded, but said nothing. He looked a little shell-shocked, to be honest. I breathed in the heady aroma of my beverage and gently took a few sips, careful not to scald my tongue. I didn't need that on top of the other injuries. Finally, I broke the silence.

"So, what's up?"

"Huh? Oh, sorry. Just thinking," he muttered.

"Regale me. I have nothing better to do."

He started to say something, then stopped. He screwed up his face, searched for the right words, had another false start.

"I shouldn't have left you," he finally said. "I know you told me not to wait around, but if I had, you wouldn't have had to walk through that alley. You wouldn't have been jumped. You wouldn't be here."

"Whoa, kid. This has nothing to do with you. I have a pretty good feeling I was going to be jumped no matter what. I think the guy was following me. If you had been there, you'd either be in here with me now... or worse."

"What, were you being stalked or something?"

"Something like that."

He fell silent again.

We sat there for a while, not talking. I'm not one of those people who feels the need to fill every moment with idle chatter —I'm comfortable with silence. So I enjoyed my coffee as Mac stared out the window, lost in thought.

After about ten minutes, I opened my mouth to say something. Mac did too; we spoke over each other. I cut my question short, then asked Mac to repeat himself.

"Where's your phone?" he asked.

"In my pants, I think."

Mac fished the phone out of my jeans, flipped it over, snapped the back off, and took out the battery. He examined the battery carefully, then replaced it.

"Okay, Gray. If that guy was following you, how did he know where to find you? Hell, even I didn't know where you were going until we got there."

I'd been wondering the same thing myself.

"Also, if this attack is connected to the one from the day before, and if they knew how and where to find you, why wait a day? Why didn't they take you out while you were asleep?"

Damn, it was like we were sharing the same brain.

"I don't know," I admitted.

Mac smiled.

"I think I do." He held up my phone.

Mac explained that all cell phones are equipped with GPS-tracking software. Even though you could keep your installed apps from using it, you couldn't disable it altogether: it was a fail-safe design for emergency responders and law enforcement. Any programmer worth his salt could track the location of any phone as long as it was powered on. It made sense as soon as he said it. My phone had been dead the whole night before the attack—there was no way anyone would have known where I was holed up—but I had put a small charge on it the next morning before heading out.

Mac handed the phone over to me, and I glared at it suspiciously.

"Guess I need a new one of these," I said.

"Yeah, but you also need a new number," Mac warned. "If you transfer your old number to a new phone, it won't matter: they can still find you. I can pick you up a cheap prepaid phone pretty much anywhere and program it with a different number."

"Okay."

Mac got up to leave. "Hang on a minute. Frank said you had some information for me. Were you able to trace that virus or whatever?"

"Oh, right." Mac sat back down. "I found the email the spyware piggy-backed on and traced it back to a local IP address."

"That sounds simple enough."

"Not exactly. It took some doing. Whoever sent it is pretty good—they routed through several servers trying to cover their tracks—but I'm better."

"That's why we pay you the big bucks."

"Right."

"So you've got an address for me?"

"Not exactly. IP addresses are only loosely tied to a geographic address. They aren't static. If I knew exactly what time the email was sent and had access to the ISP records, then I could tell you more. But I don't, so I can't."

"Okay..."

"Anyway, the email came from a location near Randolph and Halsted. I can't get any more specific than that."

The intersection of Randolph and Halsted is in West Town, a neighborhood close to downtown and within spitting distance of the Kennedy Expressway. I couldn't say what was in the vicinity off the top of my head, but it was a place to start looking.

I thanked Mac for the coffee again and decided it was time

to get up from this godforsaken adjustable bed. I pushed the button on the side rail and shifted myself so I could swing my legs over. Sharp barbs of pain lanced through my ribs as the muscles connected to them contracted. My breath caught, but the pain eased, and I was able to get to my feet.

Mac had draped my jeans over the chair. I shuffled over to them and got my wallet out of the back pocket.

"How much for a new phone?" I asked. "Nothing fancy, but I'll need access to the Internet."

"Fifty bucks will cover it," he told me.

Crap. I handed him two twenties and told him I'd give him the rest as soon as I could get to an ATM.

The stupid blue hospital gown I was wearing came untied in the back; I could feel it wafting around, exposing my nether regions. Apparently, it was making Mac uncomfortable. He grabbed the cash and told me not to worry about it—he'd add it to my bill—then muttered something about those big bucks I promised before sidling out the door.

Refusing to be ignored any longer, my bladder screamed that it was going to pop the cork in about five seconds. I made it to the bathroom just in time.

***

A couple of hours later, I was released from the hospital. Apparently they'd figured out that my insurance sucks and they couldn't milk any other charges out of the situation, so they cut me loose with a prescription for heavy-duty painkillers and strict instructions to not overexert myself.

Mac returned from his errand with my new phone and offered me a ride to wherever I needed to go.

My apartment was no longer being held as a crime scene, but if I was out to get me, that would be the first place I'd look. The office carried the same risk.

I wanted to get off the grid, so to speak. The motel I'd

90

stayed at was a good option: no one knew I'd been there, and it wasn't too expensive. Of course, I'd been wearing the same grungy clothes since this whole fiasco began five days ago. I needed to change.

Also, I no longer had a gun; it had been turned over to the cops by the hospital staff. I didn't like being without a weapon, especially not now. I'd have to pick up my spare.

I asked Mac to stop at the Public Storage facility a couple of blocks from my apartment. I rented a tiny indoor unit there to keep the stuff that I didn't have room for at home. Those cost a little more than the outdoor ones, but they kept things from rusting.

I made my way to my unit, then opened the circular lock that secured the corrugated metal door. The door swung out with a creak and banged against the facing wall, echoing down the hallway and making me flinch.

Inside the cramped space, I rearranged the boxes until I found what I was looking for: a beat-up, faded, olive drab foot locker that belonged to my grandfather during the second World War. I spun the face of the combination lock and popped it open. I'd used that same lock on my high school locker. I smiled, thinking how strange it was that I clung to something that brought back unpleasant memories every time I used it. Glutton for punishment, that's me.

I shook my head and reached into the foot locker, withdrawing an item wrapped in oilcloth: my spare weapon, a black government-issue Colt .45 semi-auto. It was a heavy, older model, made entirely of steel. It felt solid and substantial, not like the newer models made of plastic and composite materials. Its only real enemy was rust, but I kept it clean and dry and oiled it every so often to prevent any from building up.

I'd inherited this gun from my old man. He was a hard ass —guess that's where I get my attitude—and a gun collector. Actually, I'm not sure "collector" is the right term; he was more like a hoarder, with a stockpile of weapons for when "the world went to shit," which, according to him, was always about to happen. Every time a Democrat was elected, he went out and bought another gun.

Once, a few years before he died, he'd taken me into the den and pulled out the Colt. He told me he'd picked it up from a man wearing a Santa suit on Christmas Eve in a Wal-Mart parking lot in New Jersey. He also said that if I ever needed to make somebody disappear, this was the gun I should use, because if I tossed it, it would never be traced back to me. Yep, that's the kind of man my father was.

I ran my finger over the slide, where the serial number had been filed off. Carrying this particular weapon was highly illegal. Hell, just owning it was probably a felony. I'd be in a whole lot of trouble if I was caught with it. Of course, with the way my week was going, I could be a whole lot of dead if I was caught without it.

I reached back into the foot locker and pulled out the holster that went with it. Originally, my dad had paired it with an old, worn leather belt holster. Once I'd inherited it, I bought a newer nylon shoulder holster. Because of its nature, I figured it would be best to keep the pistol hidden if I ever did need to carry it. I strapped everything on and pulled my windbreaker on top, then locked up and returned to the car.

Next, I had Mac park on the first residential street behind my apartment. I went up the back stairs, hoping to avoid detection. Once inside, I moved cautiously from room to room, hand resting on the butt of the pistol at my ribs. I paused in the front room, caught off-guard by the brownish stain staring at me from the middle of the area rug. I'd have to get rid of that; blood stains didn't exactly say "Welcome to the love shack, ladies." Damn, I really liked that rug too. Did I mention it was my grandma's?

When I was sure the place was empty, I went back to the bedroom, grabbed a duffel bag from the top of my closet, and shoved clothes in. I wasn't sure how long I'd be gone, so I grabbed two pairs of jeans, three or four T-shirts, a button-up, and as many clean pairs of socks and underwear as I could fit.

I was almost to the door when I made a U-turn and grabbed my toothbrush and toothpaste. Then I hobbled back out to Mac's car, and we took off again.

This time, I had him drive a circuitous route back to the motel. I didn't think we were being followed, but I figured it wouldn't hurt to try to shake a tail.

By this time, I was in a crap ton of pain again.

Mac let me off in front of the building. Motels in Chicago have more of a European feel to them than they do elsewhere in the States. Like everything else in the city, they're narrow, multi-story structures. They don't have expansive parking lots with a sheltered car port for checking in. There might be an awning, but that's about all you get on the outside.

I went in and asked if they could move me to a ground floor room, explaining that I was recovering from an injury that made it difficult to climb stairs—which was true. They didn't have any, so they stuck me one floor up. Getting up to the room was agonizing. Getting undressed was also painful and some-what awkward. Getting my shirt off proved to be too problematic, so I left it on and gingerly slid between the sheets. Within minutes, I was sound asleep.

16

I was floating above the city again, staring down at the lights of traffic crawling through the streets below. Only it wasn't the effusive glow of headlights and taillights, I realized. It was the same red and blue energy I'd dreamed of earlier.

Though I was hundreds of feet in the air, it looked as if I could reach out and touch the pulsing cords writhing along the earth's surface. I put out a hand, noticing that it seemed translucent, ethereal. One of the blue ribbons, thicker than the others, drew me towards it. Hesitantly, I poked at it with a finger. To my surprise, the rope of light responded, curling lazily around my fingertip. Tiny chilly pinpricks dotted my flesh. It wasn't an unpleasant sensation, but enough to trigger a rush of endorphins. I left my finger there, curious to see what would happen. The light completely surrounded my finger, then the brightness around it flared to a blinding intensity and just as quickly dissipated. When my sight returned, I could see the energy flowing through my finger instead of around it. Tendrils of light coursed up my arm; my veins glowed a ghostly blue.

Startled, I withdrew my finger. The glow within me subsided, cut off from its source.

Dreams are weird, I thought.

As soon as I acknowledged it was a dream, it changed. My vision now shifted to the spectral mirror from before. Again, the city was silhouetted behind me. I stood there, trying to discern some meaning from all of this. A face drifted into focus just above my right shoulder: the cold visage of Fletcher Harrison. Now all pretense was gone from his features; only the sharp, steely gaze of a hunter remained. He scared the bejeezus out of me. His cold hazel eyes, surprisingly devoid of malice, fixed on me.

Through the looking glass, his hoarse whisper echoed in

my head, *the Jabberwock is real.*

The disembodied head shrank, retreating into the background. I glanced over my shoulder, but saw only blackness behind me. In the mirror, I could just barely make out a tiny figure, Harrison disappearing into the shadowy cityscape.

Taking a deep breath, I plunged forward, arms outstretched, remembering how the glass had rippled like water in my last dream. I hit the surface, and it gave, flexed, but resisted my movement. I lowered my head and pushed harder. The silvery material enveloped me. With a final heave, I forced myself through the mirror. The mirror shattered behind me with a loud crack, sending thousands of tiny glass shards hurtling through the air toward my back.

My eyes snapped open in the motel room. It was still completely dark. My chest heaved as I caught my breath.

Pieces of the puzzle were falling into place. I didn't like the picture it was showing, but I couldn't ignore it.

I slowly sat up, expecting to feel the now-familiar burn in my ribs. Surprisingly, all I felt was a tight soreness. I swung my feet around to the floor, carefully stood up, walked into the closet-sized bathroom, and peeled my T-shirt over my head. In the mirror over the sink, I could see the jaundice-yellow hue of old bruises peeking around where they'd taped my ribs.

I returned to the bedroom and retrieved the bandages the nurse had given me before I checked out of the hospital, with instructions to change the dressing on my neck twice a day for a week.

Back at the sink I used a warm washcloth to loosen the industrial-strength tape adhered to my skin. I'm pretty sure duct tape would have been easier to remove. The bottom layers of gauze were stained a dark brown with blood and other fluids that had leaked from the stitches, but the wound itself looked pretty good. Bright pink flesh puckered around the sutures. It wasn't swollen and showed no sign of infection. I was kind of surprised it was healing so quickly, but I'm no doctor, so what do I know?

I washed the wound as best I could with the washcloth and the little bar of complementary soap on the counter. Cucumber melon. Fancy.

Then I went and sat at the sole desk chair occupying the main room. I didn't bother putting clothes on yet—it was still dark out—so I just sat there thinking, naked as a jaybird. I had a lot to think about.

By the time the sun came up, I had a plan. Sort of. Okay, at least the outline of a plan. It was better than nothing.

Using my new phone, I called in and checked my voicemail. No new messages. That was good.

Sometimes we take all the technology surrounding us for granted. Voicemail has been around so long it's almost prehistoric, but the fact that you can call your own number from anywhere in the world, punch a few buttons, and listen to your messages in complete anonymity is pretty awesome. Especially when you're on the lam and can't answer your phone in the first place. Next, I called Frank, who was glad to hear I was up and about. I repeated my desire to keep him as uninvolved in this mess as possible, and then apologized, because I did need his help in one small matter.

I told him what I was thinking—the Spark notes version, anyway—and asked if he knew anybody who could help. Frank has way more contacts in the city than I do, since he's been doing this private eye thing a lot longer, and those contacts give him access to a lot of information. Quickly. In the detective business, it's not about how much you know, but about knowing the people who do know that gives you an edge. Sure enough, Frank did know somebody, but it would take him a few minutes to find the number. He'd call me back when he found it. I gave him my temporary number and asked him not to share it with anyone; I could still check my messages, but I was taking certain precautions. He understood, and we hung up.

I put on a fresh change of clothes and immediately felt re-energized. Clean clothes can do wonders for the soul, especially when you've been wearing the same thing for a week. I strapped on the Colt and slipped my jacket on top, making sure the pistol was well covered. I would have preferred the concealing folds of my trench coat, but I didn't have the time or inclination to pick it up from the office. Right now, I had more pressing matters.

By the time I finished dressing, the cell phone was buzzing on the desk where I'd left it. It was Frank. I jotted down the name and number he gave me. He also suggested I come by for dinner that night; apparently Nancy had been chomping at the bit to get a good home-cooked meal in me since the attack. She wasn't the kind of woman to take no for an answer when it came to feeding people. I told him I'd think about it.

"Good. See you at seven."

He hung up before I could respond. It was only eight o'-clock, still too early to call Frank's contact, so I jammed the paper into my pocket and went downstairs to the itty-bitty lobby.

I love a good hotel breakfast with waffles, eggs, sausage, and all the coffee you can drink. This wasn't a good hotel breakfast, just a few Pop-Tarts and individually wrapped cheese danishes laid out on a counter next to a toaster. I found a couple of blueberry muffins mixed in with the danishes, so I took two: one for now and one to store in my jacket pocket for later. Just in case.

At least there was coffee, although the cups were midget-sized. There wasn't any place to sit, so I ate my muffin standing at the counter while the coffee cooled. I drank the first cup in three swallows. While I was getting a refill, the desk clerk pointed out a minifridge under the counter and said there was milk and some fruit in it. So much for my incredible detective skills and powers of observation. I added a banana to the smorgasbord. After a third cup of coffee, I went outside and caught a bus headed downtown.

While I was on the bus, I called the number Frank had given me and made an appointment for later that day.

***

The Chicago Public Library is an impressive display of postmodern architecture. Encompassing an entire city block, it is the largest library building in the Unites States. Outside, it looks almost fortresslike, with giant granite blocks protruding from the street giving way to ten floors of red brick. Perched atop the roof are gargantuan metal owls which look like gargoyles from afar. Inside is a soaring grand lobby with marble floors that echo every booted footfall. And on top of its elegant grandeur, it's the best place to get free access to a computer. I could access the Internet on my new phone, but I wanted complete anonymity for what I was going to do, and the only place where I could get that was the library.

I had to wait around for a while before they let me on a PC. Once I was situated at the little cubicle, I signed up for a Gmail account with a banal username, chisoxfan1077, and made up all the personal information required. Then I navigated over to Craigslist and posted in the beauty section, advertising dreadlock services. I tried to make it read as illiterately as I could, something like *"Yo, need dread locks? I da man. Holla back."* I hoped it didn't need much substance. I wanted the right people to respond.

If and when they did, I already had a location in mind to give the kidnappers: a spot in Logan Square, a predominantly Hispanic neighborhood on the Blue Line. I had spent a lot of time there in my early twenties. There was a little Mexican place, El Cid #2, that had the best burritos in the city, oozing with queso fresco, and amazing salsa cruda. They also had margaritas the size of your face, which is the main reason I had gone there. Everything else was incidental.

The address I had in mind was laid out perfectly for an ambush, and that's exactly what I planned on doing. I needed to know more about this human trafficking organization, and the best way to get it was to question someone involved. I wasn't sure what the time frame on this little project would be, but I had other leads to track down in the meantime.

17

The nameplate beside the door read *Prof. William P. Mc-Manus, PhD.* The door stood open, so I knocked twice before sticking my head in.

I had expected a lavish space with plush carpet, a mahogany desk, and dark wood paneling on the walls. That stereotypical mental image couldn't have been further from the truth. Instead, Dr. McManus sat behind a beige metal desk littered with stacks of paper that threatened to topple over at the slightest disturbance. Austere wooden shelves lined the painted cinderblock walls and were crammed with numerous texts. The periwinkle Berber covering the floor was anything but plush.

The professor looked up from a paper he was reading and gave a toothy grin.

"Ah, you must be Mr. Gray. Please, come in."

He, too, wasn't what I had expected of someone with his reputation. Rather than the tall, lean Sherlockian demeanor I had imagined an expert in Religion and Mythology would exude, Mc-Manus was a round man of average height. A well-trimmed beard peppered with gray adorned his chin and jowls. His eyes twinkled as he spoke. As I stepped into the room, all I could think of was Santa Claus.

"Sit down, sit down," he beamed.

"I'm glad you could meet on such short notice," I said as I settled into a wooden chair across from him. "Frank said you were the expert I needed."

It was 1:05 in the afternoon. After my trip to the library, it had taken me almost two hours to get to Evanston on the Red Line and then a cab to Northwestern University.

"Not a problem. I don't get too many students during office hours, so I'm glad for a break from all these term papers." He flicked the paper he was holding and grinned at me as he set it down on a stack in front of him. He removed his glasses and asked, "So what brings you here today? I must admit, I'm quite curious to know how my studies could assist with your line of work."

I didn't want to sound crazy, so I tried to explain as best as I could.

"The case I'm working on has brought me into contact with... peculiar individuals. I have very strong reason to believe that they may be part of a cult that fancies themselves to be vampires. I need to be able to predict their behavior, to identify weaknesses in their routines and beliefs that I could exploit."

"I see," he replied. "You are aware that my expertise is historical in nature and not of modern fantasy?"

"Yes, sir. I'm hoping that if I can learn the commonalities that exist across the mythology, it will give me a basic understanding of this group that I can flesh out as I learn more details about them specifically." The professor nodded his head, clutching the earpiece of his glasses in his teeth.

"I like your thinking," he said. "Yes, that sounds like a good thesis paper for one of my students." He chuckled to himself. "Sorry, teaching on the brain. I would think, that, in our culture, they would stick to the traditional vampire archetype popularized by Bram Stoker's *Dracula*, which has its roots in Romanian folklore. Even modern vampire stories are descendants of that tale, albeit each with their own twists and embellishments."

"Are there other vampire legends before Dracula?" I asked.

"Most certainly. In fact, there is vampire mythology from nearly every culture around the globe. The earliest on record dates back to the early Persian empire around 500 BC. Of course, they weren't called vampires. They had a wide variety of names, including demons and devils. Some even claim the ancient Lilith was the first vampire. But whatever they were called, they share many of the same characteristics, which is what you are after—am I right?"

"Yep."

"Okay, let's think about this. The most basic thing all the legends have in common is that they subsist on the life force of others, usually by drinking their blood." McManus paused to gather his thoughts. "The only other thing I can think of that applies across the board is that they have some level of immortality —they're either raised from the dead or are of demonic origin."

"That's not much to go on," I said. Had this trip been a waste of time?

"No, not really," McManus agreed, "but let me rethink the parameters. Let's begin with the Romanian folklore and cross-reference that with other legends and myths to see if any patterns emerge."

"All right."

He placed his glasses on the desk, leaned back in his chair, and steepled his fingers. "Okay, I think we can do away with the shape-shifting powers—no turning into bats or wolves—but most, though not all, of the stories I'm familiar with allude to the creatures' nocturnal nature. There's also a thread of charismatic hypnosis that manifests in different ways."

"What do you mean by that?"

"Well, Dracula could stare into his victim's eyes and lull them into a hypnotic trance. Other references assign these creatures the ability to cast spells that bend the will of others. But the most ancient texts simply describe them as charismatic. Despite popular belief, most of the demons characterized in religious texts are portrayed not as hideous monsters that rule through fear, but rather as beautiful creatures who appeal to our vanity and sense of self."

"Hmmm," I mused. "That explains the sexy vampire trend of late."

"Indeed."

"What about lacking a reflection, sleeping in a coffin, being allergic to garlic... that sort of thing?"

"Most of that lore is relatively modern, I'm afraid. There doesn't seem to be any historical basis for it. Although most of these creatures are said to have some weakness to silver."

Silver. Every dark cloud has a silver lining. Interesting.

I pushed the conversation a little further.

"Do you think these stories have any basis in fact? Could there actually have been a vampire-like creature in the past?"

The professor's eyes twinkled. He picked up his spectacles and twirled them between his fingers.

"That, Mr. Gray, is the question we would all like answered."

McManus spent the next twenty minutes regaling me with his theories about the origins of vampire stories and other myths and legends. I had opened a can of worms, it seemed, and he was delighted to have a captive audience.

The short of it was that, yes, he did believe that these legends had some root in fact. Most legends did, he said, but they had been exaggerated and twisted over the years until they took on a life on their own.

Manatees, for example, were the basis for stories about mermaids, giant squids gave rise to the tale of the Kraken, and people who contracted rabies may have been construed as werewolves. Of course, the origins of many myths were still shrouded in mystery, either because the legend bore no resemblance to its historical counterpart or because whatever had inspired it no longer existed. As for vampires, McManus felt they were an iteration of ancient demons who may have been an explanation for some disease or other.

I finally excused myself, thanked him for his time and expertise, and saw myself out of the University.

The stores didn't close for another couple of hours, so I made my way back downtown. I wanted to scope out the area in West Town to which Mac had traced the virus-containing email. If people were still on the streets, I could snoop around without attracting attention. Plus, I'd be that much closer to Frank's when dinnertime rolled around.

Randolph and Halsted is a busy intersection. There are several bars and restaurants, some stores, and a bank or two at ground level and apartments on the upper floors. I wasn't sure what I was looking for, exactly, but I at least wanted to get the lay of the land.

I walked north on Halsted, pondering what type of place a human trafficker would use to shelter the people he abducted. It would have to be unobtrusive: hidden in plain sight, perhaps, but out of the way, where no one would stumble upon it. It would need to be quiet, too, or at least soundproof. Of course, an email could have been sent from just about anywhere; I wasn't necessarily looking for a slaver's hideout. An idea popped into my head at the sight of a boutique real estate place. I needed to narrow my search, and I thought I knew where to start.

The place was called Shabby Chic Real Estate. Behind the counter sat a curvy brunette typing on a computer. She was young, maybe in her mid-twenties, and wore a forest green jacket over a white blouse with a wide collar. She looked up when I entered and smiled, but the smile didn't reach her eyes.

"Hello. How can I help you today?" she asked.

"Hi..." I glanced at the nameplate on the counter. "Brenda. I have a couple of questions about listings in the neighborhood. I could come back tomorrow if you're about to close up."

"I'm here until six," she said.

"Could you pull up a list of all the buildings for sale or rent in a one block radius around Randolph and Halsted?"

She looked at me funny.

"I know it's kind of specific, but as they say, location, location, location."

"All right. Commercial or residential?"

"Both."

She gave me another funny look.

I shrugged and said, "I like to work close to home."

I could tell she didn't buy my lie at all, but she humored me anyway, clicking her mouse several times. A nearby printer whirred to life, feeding out several sheets of paper. She stood and grabbed them off the tray and picked up a pen.

"The computer can't limit the search exactly within those boundaries, but I'll cross off anything that's outside your search area." She read over the pages and marked through a couple of listings.

"You know this area pretty well, I take it?"

"I suppose so. Why?"

"Know of anyone in the area who would be interested in selling or renting but hasn't listed?"

"Um... maybe," she said, squinting in thought. She eyed me up and down. "Are you really interested in buying something?"

I should have answered with an emphatic "Of course," but I hesitated.

One thing you discover quickly in my line of work is that if someone hesitates before answering a simple question and then gives the "right" answer, they're usually lying. Even if you don't consciously pick up on the fact that you've just been lied to, your brain still gets it. Suspicion is automatically aroused; what they said just feels wrong.

For some reason, a gut feeling, I wanted this woman to trust me... and my gut was usually right.

"Actually, no," I admitted.

She narrowed her eyes.

"I am looking for a place in the neighborhood, but it's not for me." I lowered my voice to a conspiratorial tone. "I'm a private investigator. I'm looking for someone who may be hiding out in this area. I have an idea of the type of place they might be, and I was hoping you could help me narrow my search."

Brenda glanced down the hallway, where I imagined the actual realtors had offices, and lowered her voice as well. "I don't know how much help I'll be, but I can try."

I filled her in on the kind of place I was looking for. It was most likely not on the market, but was vacant or used for storage. Her eyes widened, and she took half a step back.

Just then, a door opened down the hallway. Brenda looked over her shoulder again, then met my eyes once more.

"I'm sorry, sir," she said in an even but slightly louder tone, "but we don't currently have any properties that fit those parameters. If your requirements change at all, please give us a call at this number." She scribbled something onto one of the printouts and handed me the stack of papers. We made eye contact again, and this time she held it. Her eyebrows arched a smidge; she firmly gripped the papers.

I nodded just a bit. Her face relaxed, and she let go.

"Thanks for stopping in," she said, and returned to her computer. I turned and walked out the door. Outside, I glanced down at the paperwork and saw not a phone number, but an address. Weird. Brenda wanted to tell me something, but for whatever reason didn't feel comfortable doing so in the office.

***

It was only five thirty, so the little bar on the corner was mostly empty. I found a table by a window where I could keep an eye on the real estate place, ordered a gin and tonic, and waited.

The address written on the paper wasn't in the neighborhood, so I wasn't sure what to make of it. I wanted to talk to Brenda again, to figure out what she wanted to tell me.

A few minutes after six, she left the office and locked the door behind her. She walked past the bar and stopped just shy of the corner at the bus stop. While she waited, she looked around nervously, finally glancing across the street in my direction.

Her gaze stopped roving when she saw me. I laid a ten on the table, then pushed back my chair to get up, but she slowly shook her head, warning me off.

A minute later, the bus pulled up, and she got on. As it drove away, a beat-up black Ford Taurus with tinted windows pulled away from the curb and followed it.

I hurried from the bar and stood on the sidewalk to get a better look. Instead of passing the bus, the car slowed down when it made its next stop. It appeared my receptionist friend had a tail. I decided to tail the tail, and I flagged down the next cab that came by.

It only took a couple of blocks to catch up, as the bus seemed to be stopping at every intersection, with the Taurus still easing along behind it. I had the cabbie pull over: I wanted to stay far enough back that they wouldn't notice me, but close enough that I could see when Brenda got off.

While we were stopped, I punched the address she had given me into my phone and saw that it was about two miles south of where we were now. I figured that's where she was headed. I was tempted to have the cab take me straight there, but I didn't like the way she was being followed, and I had no time frame on when she'd arrive, so I figured I'd better keep watching.

Sure enough, Brenda got off the bus a couple of miles down, then headed west. The Taurus turned and drove past her; she watched it carefully. It was a wide boulevard with a decent amount of traffic so I figured my cab wouldn't be noticed. I had the driver keep following the Taurus. It parked on the north side of the road about two blocks down, across from a large brick apartment building. I told the cabbie to keep driving and turn right at the next street, then had him drop me off. Not knowing how long this would take, I paid him and sent him on his way.

I walked back to the corner to get a peek at the car. By this point, the driver, a slick-looking guy wearing a black topcoat and sunglasses, had gotten out and was leaning against the driver's side door. Brenda made her way down the other side of the street, going out of her way not to look at him.

She let herself in through a wrought-iron gate that opened onto a grassy courtyard and proceeded into the building.

I hung out on the corner, waiting to see if Slick would follow her in. He didn't. He lit up a cigarette and stood there, glaring at the apartment building. I followed suit, because no one would think twice about some guy hanging out on the corner for a smoke break. When the guy finished his cigarette, he got back into the car and peeled off. I lingered a few more minutes to make sure he didn't double back, then crushed the butt of mine on the sidewalk with my heel.

I casually strolled back the way I had come and crossed the street. The gate to the courtyard had a busted lock, and it opened with a gentle push. The building's front door was a different story. It was sturdy with a fully functional deadbolt. After a quick inspection I decided that I could force it open if need be, but what was the point? I had an address with me, and there were buzzers.

I found the correct button, labeled 3E, and pressed it.

A crackly voice came over the tiny speaker. "Hello."

"I think I found something that belongs to you," I said. "It's a piece of paper with this address on it. I think it's important."

There was a brief pause, then a loud buzz as the door lock disengaged.

18

"Come in," said Brenda as she cautiously opened the door, glancing up and down the hallway.

"He's gone," I assured her, and stepped into the small one-bedroom unit.

A little boy, about two or three, sat on a couch to the left of the door in the living room. He was completely engrossed in some cartoon playing on an older tube-style TV, oblivious to my presence.

The apartment was small but well-kept, its furnishings sparse but tasteful, and the place had a warm, homey feel. An apartment in the city was expensive, especially for a single mother—I didn't see any sign of a man living here—but Brenda clearly took pride in her little abode.

"Coffee?" she asked.

"Sure," I replied, and took another step inside.

She gestured to a small table just in front of the doorway that led to the kitchen, then busied herself making a pot of fresh coffee. I took a seat and waited. For some reason, I got the feeling our conversation wasn't going to begin until the coffee was served, and it didn't feel right to push it.

Eventually, she placed a heavy cup in front of me and settled herself in the chair across the table with her own cup. I took a tentative sip. It was remarkably good.

"So," she began. "I'm sorry I couldn't talk at the office. Things there are... complicated."

"They usually are," I said. "Why are you being followed?"

She pressed her lips into a thin line. "They don't want me talking to anyone about what's going on. Did they see you come in here?"

"No, I made sure your tail was gone first. So, what's going on?"

"I'm not sure where to begin." She sipped her coffee while gathering her thoughts. "I've noticed a lot of inconsistencies in business deals. We've sold certain properties to small companies that quickly go broke. Once they're foreclosed on, we swoop in and repurchase the property at a substantially reduced price, only to sell them again. But I think the small businesses are actually subsidiaries of our company whose only purpose is to go broke. We also offer financing options with adjustable rates that crank up ridiculously high after a few months."

Swindling the banks and predatory lending. How delightful. Brenda was working for some real winners.

"Do you have any evidence?" I asked.

"Lots, but I can't take it anywhere. They've threatened me and Benjamin." She looked toward her son and sighed. "I don't want to be a part of this anymore, but I don't know what to do. These people are scary. I thought my boss was bad, but then *his* boss showed up yesterday, and..." She shivered.

I took another swig and watched her over the brim of my mug.

"Maybe we can help each other out?" I offered. She perked up.

"I get the feeling you can point me toward the kind of place I mentioned earlier, that maybe you know exactly what I'm looking for, and I have a friend on the force who I could talk to about your employer."

"Really? You'd do that?"

"Of course. Let's start with the threats they've made."

Brenda explained that she'd received pictures of her son at his daycare and that she'd been warned to keep quiet unless she wanted to lose everything. She was afraid that someone working at the daycare was connected to her employer, since they'd recommended it. The man I'd seen in the Taurus had followed her every day for several months, though he'd made no overt contact.

Whoever these people were, it sounded like they were organized and had planned for her discoveries well in advance of hiring her. I doubt they had targeted her specifically, but she fit a certain profile: a single mother who desperately needed a good job and could be easily intimidated into keeping her mouth shut. The whole situation pissed me off.

Then Brenda told me about the properties the company owned. They had their fingers on industrial lots scattered around the city, but one in particular seemed to fit the bill: a small warehouse in West Town near the office that, by all accounts, should have been listed and sold or leased long ago, because it would have turned a very hefty profit. And yet it sat vacant. To her knowledge, they didn't use it for anything, but she'd never been inside. It sounded like the perfect place to hold kidnapping victims until they could be transported elsewhere. I had to check it out.

"All right," I said when she seemed talked out. "Let me make a phone call and see what I can work out."

I thumbed my phone on and saw that I had a new email on the account I'd set up earlier. I'd check that later. Then I called Mac. After a brief chat, I had enough information to advise Brenda on her next move.

"Okay, Brenda, here's what I want you to do. Go to work tomorrow like normal. You'll get an email sometime in the morning with 'graystone three-bedroom' in the subject line. It will contain several .jpeg files as attachments. Open them all. They'll be encoded with a Trojan horse that will give my friend remote access to your system so that he can image the hard drive. That way, we can get copies of all the incriminating files without putting you at risk of discovery. Even if your bosses wipe the system, we'll still have everything. Tomorrow night, I'll send someone to take you and your son someplace safe. His name is

Frank. Think you can handle that?"

"Yes," she replied. "Thank you so much."

"No problem." I checked my watch: it was almost seven. I was going to be late for dinner. "Now, I need to get back to another project. Is there a back exit I can use?"

She showed me out and directed me to a back door.

***

While I waited for a cab, I checked my email. Sure enough, I had a reply to my Craigslist post. *Red Dreadlocks?* was all it said. I wrote a reply: *Yeah, that's right. There's an alley behind the Subway at Kedzie and Diversey. You can only get there from Sawyer Ave. Appointment at 10pm. $50. Cash only.* If Frank could give me a lift after dinner, I should have plenty of time to get there.

Frank and his family lived in Roscoe Village, a nice residential neighborhood on the Northside, on a cozy, tree-lined street. It wasn't the fanciest house, but it suited them well. It was what I'd call quaint and felt like home.

Maggie, one of their two girls, was peering out the window when I arrived. Her face disappeared as soon as she saw me, and the door swung open, revealing her small body silhouetted in the doorway with hands on her hips. Even for eight years old, she was petite.

"You're late," she said with a scowl as I climbed up to the porch.

"I know," I replied. "Something came up."

The scowl evaporated, and her face split into a wide grin. "Oh well, you're here now." She whipped around and pranced into the foyer. "Mom's not happy, though."

I followed her down the hallway into the dining room. Frank sat at the end of the table, facing me and staring at the empty plate in front of him hungrily.

As I entered, he looked up and said, "It's about damn time, Gray. Nancy! He's here!"

Nancy bustled in from the kitchen, a covered dish in hand. She set it on the table, gave me the once-over, and clucked her tongue.

"Girls! Help me get dinner on the table," she called. Then to me, she added, "Have a seat. You can help clear the dishes when we're through."

Frank's other daughter came downstairs, removing a pair of earbuds. Alice was thirteen and into all the things a typical thirteen-year-old girl is into. I don't know many of them, but she seemed normal and had friends, so that was my assumption. She's a sweet girl, and had never exhibited her little sister's attitude, but she was also a teenager and had started to distance herself from us stodgy old farts. Dinner was soon on the table, and we all dug in.

Nancy is an amazing cook. She had made meatloaf, mashed potatoes, and creamed peas, all from scratch. I know what you're thinking: *Creamed peas?* Yeah, creamed peas. They were delicious, just like my grandma used to make. It's no wonder Frank kept putting on weight. I would too if I came home to meals like that every night.

We stuck to idle chatter while the girls were at the table, ignoring the weightier issues. Soon, however, they finished eating and scampered off to watch TV or play on the Internet, and we were left alone.

"You've been busy," Frank finally said.

"Yeah," I agreed.

"Learn anything important?"

"Maybe." After the last several days, part of me felt like I was going crazy. I needed to talk to somebody, to get it off my chest. "I know what I'm about to tell you is going to sound ridiculous, but I need a sounding board."

"Gray, half the things you say sound nuts. We've never judged you before," Frank said. He chortled at his own joke.

"After you left the hospital, I had another visitor," I began, then told them about Harrison and the strange things he'd said. I moved onto my conversation with McManus and his theory that the things that go bump in the night are based on reality. I told them about the dreams I'd had, the red and blue lights, and how quickly my injuries were healing. Nancy, who had been a nurse before the girls were born, asked to see them, so I obliged. She agreed that my wounds looked far better than they should.

"That's crazy, right?" I said. "Dreams can't make you heal faster."

They looked at each other but didn't say anything.

"I'm not sure what to believe anymore," I confessed.

Frank stared hard at me for a long time, then said, "Bah, you're not crazy."

"So you believe in this vampire stuff?" I asked incredulously.

"No," he admitted, "But a whole lot of people don't believe in God, either, and I know they're wrong." He pushed his chair back, picked up his plate, and stood. "Trust your gut, Gray, just like you've always done."

Trust my gut. I knew how to do that.

I gathered my own dishes and followed him into the kitchen.

"There's one other thing I need you to help me with," I continued. I told him about Brenda and her son. Frank agreed to pick them up the next evening and deliver them to the hotel where I'd been staying. I'd crash at the office, or maybe back at my place. I was tired of being displaced.

We finished clearing the table, and I asked for a lift to Logan Square.

"I have another appointment," I informed him.

He rolled his eyes, but grabbed his car keys and said, "Come on, then."

19

I had Frank drop me off at the Walgreens in Logan Square so I could pick up a couple of things. I wasn't sure who'd show up tonight, but I had some questions that needed answering, and a roll of duct tape and a pack of zip ties could help make sure I had time to do things right. Frank offered to help, but I told him that he was absolutely not to get involved in any of this. He reluctantly agreed and drove home.

After that, I made my way to the alley where I planned to make my ambush. I'd chosen this location for a reason. Most alleys in the city are small cut-throughs between bigger streets to allow access to garages and for sanitation purposes. This one, however, didn't have an outlet. It ran from a small residential street toward Kedzie, but dead-ended behind a commercial building. There was only one way in and one way out.

Here I could situate myself so that I could see anyone going into the alley and cut them off before they left. Also, I knew there would be no through traffic, and prying eyes would be at a minimum. And what's more, one of the buildings the alley ran by was an old bar under renovation. If it came to it, I could always take the interrogation inside.

Across from the mouth of the alley was a porch stoop with several strategically placed bushes that would provide adequate concealment, but still allow me to watch the street. I hunkered down behind the bushes and leaned against the wall, then silenced my phone and checked the time: 9:36. Looked like I might be here a while.

***

Once more I was gliding above the city. The red and blue cords undulated below. I remembered how the blue energy had responded the last time, so I decided to try the red. I extended my arm and, instead of poking tentatively, plunged my entire hand into the center of a red ribbon.

At first, the light recoiled from my presence as though startled, as if it were somehow sentient, but then it attempted to resume its course. As soon as it touched my flesh, it flared brilliantly, imparting an intense heat. It rushed into my fingers and up the back of my hand.

I watched as the writhing streams of light swirled through my flesh, coalescing into an image: a picture of Brenda. A stab of anger hit my chest as I thought about her plight. The lights swirled again, this time taking on her son's youthful face. The threats against him flashed like neon signs, and my righteous anger grew, filling me completely. I clenched my fist, removing it from the stream, and let out a savage yell as the anger poured forth.

***

My eyes snapped open, and my chest heaved as I caught my breath. I was pissed as hell and struggled to rein it in. Across the darkened street, I caught a glimpse of movement entering the alley.

I clamped down on my rage and let it seethe just below the surface. Eyes scanning the shadows, I sprang to my feet from the hiding spot and strode across the street into the alley. I made out the outline of a person ahead. As I got closer, I saw he was wearing an army surplus jacket with his hands stuffed in the pockets. He was about four inches shorter than me and kind of scrawny, but a gun could level the playing field pretty quick, so I picked up the pace to close the distance.

I crunched some loose gravel. The guy looked over his shoulder and turned to face me.

He stuck out his chin and said, "You the dreadlock guy?"

That was all the evidence I needed.

I surged forward, covering the last few yards between us

before he could react. I extended my arms and grabbed the front of his jacket, then stepped past him using that forward momentum—twisting my hips, pulling with my arms, pivoting on my right foot—and heaved for all I was worth.

The result was beautiful.

His feet left the ground, and we spun in a broad arc like two ballroom dancers. He let out a loud "oomph" as his back slammed into the brick wall. His eyes lost focus, going glassy for a second, and then he sucked in a deep breath and sputtered.

"You have one chance to answer my questions," I growled.

"Yeah, man, whatever. I know stuff, but it wasn't me. I swear." The guy had broken out in a sweat. His pupils were dilated, and I thought I smelled a hint of urine. Did I just make this guy piss himself? Part of my brain wanted to laugh, but that part was currently buried under a much bigger and louder part that was screaming for me to rip his head off.

"Tell me what you know," I hissed through clenched teeth.

"It was Gerald's idea. I told him it was no good. I had nothing to do with it, I swear."

I had no idea what he was talking about, but I decided to roll with it.

"How do you know?"

"He came to me and said he had an idea. Said we could pocket some of the cash, and nobody would be the wiser. Said the way you guys paid us, under the table and all, there weren't no records being kept. Nobody'd ever find out. I told him it was crap and wasn't gonna do it. I want to join one day, and I wasn't going to risk it."

This rat wanted to join these kidnappers? The anger surged through me again, and my jaw clenched.

"Join," I barked. "Why would you want to join?"

"Because," the man stuttered. "Look at you. Look how

strong you are." He cut his eyes toward the ground. "I want that. I'll do whatever it takes."

Only then did I glance down. The guy's feet were a good eighteen inches off the ground; I was holding him pinned against the wall like it was nothing. Small as he was, he had to weigh at least one-eighty, but it didn't feel like it. I could have been hold-ing a teddy bear against the wall. How the hell was I doing that? Adrenaline?

The realization hit me like a smack in the face. I dropped him as my anger faded into confusion.

"Where do you take them?" I asked.

"What?" His eyes narrowed, and his expression turned sour. "Who are you?"

"A bigger threat than anyone else at the moment," I replied.

Senses heightened, I felt, more than saw, him pull some-thing from his right pocket. I didn't know what it was, but I was-n't taking any chances. Still holding the front of his jacket, I was too close to step away and draw my own weapon so I rammed my forehead into his face.

Blood exploded from his nose, and he fumbled whatever he held in his hand.

I took half a step back, seized his right wrist with my right hand, and pulled it across his body, half turning him in his mo-mentary daze. I grabbed the back of his shoulder with my other hand and forced him the rest of the way around, then I yanked his arm up behind his back in the old "say uncle" pose.

He was still desperately trying to hang onto some funny looking syringe.

"What's this?" I asked.

He moaned.

I plucked the syringe from his hand, then leaned into his back so he couldn't move.

"Let me guess: this is some pharmaceutical cocktail that makes a would-be kidnapping victim easy to deal with. Probably a combo of some benzodiazepine and Ketamine. It doesn't knock them out completely, right? Because then you'd have to carry them wherever, and you don't have a vehicle nearby. But once it kicks in, you can herd 'em anywhere you want." The anger had returned, but this time it was a white, cold, calculating anger instead of the red-hot rage from before. "Sounds like a good time. Want to try?"

He squirmed, but I had him pinned good. He wasn't going anywhere. I torqued on his arm a little, and he relaxed enough that I could jab the needle into the meaty part where the neck joins the shoulder.

After a few minutes, he sagged, all the fight washed away. I released my hold, and he stood there, staring at the wall.

"Hey," I said. "What's your name?"

"Louis," he answered calmly. "People call me Jonesy, though."

"All right, Jonesy, turn around." He did. "Come with me."

I led him down the alley to the back entrance of the pub that was being remodeled. I had him wait by the door, which he did without complaint. Whatever drugs those were sure did the job. I picked the lock in less than a minute and took him inside.

The interior was covered with bits of plaster and sawdust. Chairs had been stacked on tables and covered with plastic. I pulled a chair down, placed it in front of an exposed stud where they hadn't hung sheet rock yet, and sat him down. I zip tied his arms around the two-by-four, then secured his ankles. He might not want to go anywhere at the moment, but I wasn't taking any chances.

"What's going on, man?" he asked.

"We're just going to have a little conversation. Is that okay?"

"Sure." He was high as a kite.

I grabbed another chair and put it in front of him, then I straddled it. "Tell me about your job."

"It's crap, man. $8 an hour to wax down cars. No benefits..."

"That's not the job I'm talking about. Tell me about the red dreadlocks."

He stared off into space for minute. "I'm not supposed to talk about that."

"I know. But you can talk to me about it," I assured him.

"Yeah, okay. I get a text with an address or an intersection. I show up and find a homeless person. I give them the shot, then take them to the drop-off point. They give me $50."

"Where's the drop off point?" I asked.

"Menards parking lot." That had promise.

"How do you find them?"

"I text them when I've got the package. When I show up, there's a gray van parked in the back of the lot."

"Who's 'they'? Who are you working for?"

He stared for another minute. "They call themselves Red Dread." His expression turned dreamy.

"You said earlier that they were really strong. Tell me about that."

"Super strong—like mutant superhero kind of strong. And fast. Like you. It must be totally awesome to have that kind of power."

This just kept getting better and better. My skeptical nature dug in its claws, not wanting to be dragged down the rabbit hole, but it was a lost cause. I'd seen too much, and after my encounter with Harrison, I'd had a feeling I'd end up here anyway. It was time to take the red pill and see how deep this hole went.

"Are they vampires, Jonesy?"

"I don't know," he admitted. "Maybe. Could be."

"How many of them are there?"

"I don't know that either. I've only met two. But rumor has it there's a lot more. And they're looking for new members."

I sat back and thought. I had a couple of options at this point.

First option: take Jonesy to Menards and hand him off as a "package," then follow the van and see where it went. On the surface, it seemed like a decent plan. I could call them over with a text from Jonesy's phone, and it would get me a lot closer to the real bad guys. But I didn't like it. There were too many variables. I had no idea how long this sedative would last, and we'd been chatting for several minutes. What if it wore off before we got there? Plus, they might recognize Jonesy on the hand-off, and the whole thing would blow up in my face.

Second option: I could bide my time and try to join up with this crew, since they were looking for new members. That was no good either. I didn't have that kind of time if I wanted to find Ellie alive.

Third option: I send the text, then show up to observe from a distance. When the drop-off didn't show, they would leave, and I could still follow them back to their hideout. I liked that idea. Even if it didn't pan out, at least now I knew for sure that the McCarthy case, the attempts on my life, and the human trafficking ring were inextricably linked.

Now, what to do with Jonesy?

I stood and paced back and forth. Jonesy just sat there. Odds were, he wouldn't remember this conversation, but I didn't want to risk him running back to his employers and telling them I was onto them.

I looked around the bar. There were some tools scattered around: pry bars, nail guns, things that someone might steal, but in his current state, nobody would think Jonesy was capable of hauling them away. Sure, he was trespassing, but if that's all the cops found, they wouldn't even arrest him. I had to find a different angle.

I walked behind him and rifled through his jacket pockets, hoping he was carrying some contraband. All I found was his cell phone. I cut him loose and stood him up. He had $100 in cash in his wallet, so I took that and put the wallet back. No sense in letting him profit from attempted kidnapping. I took the car keys from the front pocket of his jeans, too.

I could give him my gun. That would definitely get him locked up, but I wasn't willing to part with it.

Then there was the knife I had just used to sever the zip ties. It's one of those big foldable lockback ones. That could work. It would need to look like he'd used it though. I briefly considered cutting myself to make it look bloodied, then I remembered I didn't need to: blood was still leaking from Jonesy's nose.

I found a rag and mopped some blood from his face, then smeared it along the blade. I wiped my prints off the handle and shoved it into his hand. He looked at it, then looked at me.

"It's yours," I told him. "You keep it."

He looked at it again with renewed, if detached, interest. I plopped him back on the chair, then dialed 911.

***

Menards is a common big-box hardware store in the Midwest. The one in Chicago is in a part of town with no convenient access by the Blue Line, the train that serves Logan Square. To get there via public transportation, I'd have to make a couple of transfers, which would simply take too long.

I considered taking Jonesy's car, if I could find it, but decided against it: auto theft wasn't really my style, and I didn't need the cops finding me with a stolen vehicle. So it was taxi time again. After this week, I was starting to reconsider my decision to not own a car. I might have to do something about that.

The store would be closed by now, and the parking lot

was probably pretty empty. It should be easy to spot the van I was looking for. Of course, cruising around the lot in a taxi would be pretty conspicuous as well.

I had my driver do a loop around the store on the frontage road while I scanned the parking lot. Other cars were scattered around, probably taking advantage of free parking while having a late dinner at a restaurant nearby. Sure enough, I spotted a gray van parked underneath a small tree. No other cars fit the description, so I assumed this was the van I was looking for.

We pulled into the Taco Bell parking lot across the street and sat there, waiting. It's amazing how much cab drivers will do without asking questions when they're on the clock. As long as it doesn't require anything outright illegal, they generally leave me alone and let me do whatever needs doing. Occasionally, I'll get a talker who wants to know everything I'm doing and why, but it's mostly out of curiosity and boredom. Tonight's guy was busy playing with some gadget and left me alone.

I wasn't sure how long I'd have to wait. I figured these traffickers had to get a no-show every now and then, but traffic in the city can be a beast, so it was risky to wait them out in the cab. If they took too long, I'd have to come up with another plan. I only had so much cash to play with.

My worries turned out to be unfounded. After only fifteen minutes, the van lurched into reverse and backed out of the parking spot. I tapped the driver's shoulder to get his attention and told him to get ready.

As the van made its way to the lot exit, I told the cabbie I wanted to follow it, but not too close. All we had to do was keep it in sight. I just wanted to see where it was going, not to catch them.

We waited until the van had pulled onto Clybourn Avenue and headed southeast, passing us in the process, then we pulled out of the Taco Bell lot and headed in the same direction. After several blocks, the van turned right onto Ashland, heading due south.

It was almost midnight and traffic was light. Chicago's streets are never completely empty—the city has too many people on too many different schedules for that to happen—but there are times when traffic isn't a concern. Between the hours of two and five in the morning are the quietest, but even now, we made good time as we crossed the river and neared the Expressway.

The van turned again, and I knew it was going for the on-ramp. I wasn't sure what to make of that. I had hoped these guys were local, but if they got on the Kennedy instead of staying on the surface streets, that might mean they were going somewhere far away. I glanced into the front of the cab and saw a card reader. If this went on for too much longer, at least I could pay with credit.

The city zipped by outside the windows as we picked up speed. The van was pretty far ahead of us now, staying just a little over the speed limit. I told the driver to keep this distance, and we sped toward downtown.

Before long, the van signaled and merged onto an exit: Randolph Street. Well, that was interesting. We did likewise, but by the time we got to the bottom of the ramp, we caught a red light. I rolled the window down and stuck my head out, trying to spot the van. I saw nothing to the left, so I slid over to the other side of the cab and did the same thing. Several blocks down, it swung a wide right to head back north, then disappeared.

I wondered if I'd been made, but didn't have time to dwell on it.

"Take a right! Now!" I shouted at the cabbie, a little too forcefully.

He did, but it was too late. By the time we got to the street where the van had turned, it had disappeared. We cruised down the road slowly while I peered down each cross street and alley, but it was no use. We'd lost them.

I wasn't upset; in fact, I felt pretty pleased. While it would have been nice to know exactly where they'd gone, I had enough information already. The street we'd turned onto was the same as in the warehouse address Brenda had given me earlier. I was on the right track.

I sat back and told the driver to take me to the nearest Red Line stop.

20

I was back at the Deluxe Diner in my usual spot. It was incredibly late, and I wanted nothing more than to go across the street, slide between the threadbare sheets of my own bed, and sleep until Thursday, but I had too many thoughts running through my brain.

I pulled out my notebook and started scribbling, trying to connect the dots. What I knew for sure was that a group of human traffickers was kidnapping homeless people for some unknown purpose. The group called themselves Red Dread, according to the schmuck who had been running errands, and they had supernatural strength and speed. One of them had tried to kill me, so I could vouch for that. The whole fangs-and-neck-biting thing screamed vampire, but if there were actually vampires running around the city, why was I just now finding this out? Why wasn't it all over the papers and on TMZ and crap?

Oh, right. That would be crazy. There was no evidence other than what I'd seen to support such a claim. There were no bodies at the morgue drained of blood. No video had been captured—at least, none that had been released. There was more hard evidence out there to support the existence of Bigfoot. And yet...

Back to what I knew. Ellie McCarthy, fiancée to Alderman Juarez, was missing. She might have been taken by this Red Dread group, but I wasn't sure. There was a real estate company in West Town involved in some sketchy dealings. They owned a warehouse where someone could, potentially, house people they'd kidnapped before handing them off to a buyer. I'd followed Jonesy's delivery van to the same neighborhood just a short while ago.

What I had was pretty thin, but then again, it was a hell of a lot more than what I'd had the last time I sat in this booth.

I needed a plan.

I wanted to get a look at the warehouse. I could poke around there tomorrow.

I also couldn't ignore this whole vampire thing. The pieces fit together. It made sense that something intelligent would be able to hide in plain sight if it looked just like everyone else. But I still struggled to accept it. I had to change the way I was thinking about it, let go of my assumptions about what was impossible.

I could accept that there were plenty of undiscovered things out there. I could accept that drugs and viruses could have some pretty crazy effects on the human body. But I'd emptied a magazine full of bullets into a guy with incredible strength who had apparently gotten up and walked away like I'd peppered him with a paintball gun. Yep, that was what I was having trouble accepting.

Okay, Gray. It happened, I told myself. Deal with it. But what does it mean? It means that there are people out there who can take a lot of punishment before they go down. I can accept that. Maybe they aren't vampires in the traditional, supernatural sense. Professor McManus said there were stories of vampire-like beings thousands of years before anyone came up with the word. Maybe it's a genetic mutation. Yeah, I can roll with that. Maybe that same mutation causes them to have an allergic reaction to silver. Sure, sounds reasonable.

I finished my cup of coffee and crossed the street to my apartment, where I poured myself a nice big glass of gin, drained it, and crawled into bed.

***

I dragged myself out of bed at about 10 o'clock the next morning. It was time to start checking things off my to-do list.

My first stop was a little antique store a couple of blocks from the apartment. It was really more of a junk shop, but I figured I could find some old silver for relatively cheap. I was right. They had a stash of old silver coins, mostly dimes and quarters, so worn that they were little more than silver discs. After a bit of haggling, I bought them for just over scrap price.

Next, I hit the storage locker again and dug up my dad's old reloading stuff. Being a collector, he'd refused to waste spent brass and had amassed a wide variety of calibers. I'm not sure why I'd kept it all, but it sure was going to come in handy now. It took me a few minutes to put my hands on what I needed, but I emerged from my hoard with a press, scales, the right die, and a mold for .45-caliber bullets.

The next step was to get all this stuff to the office; I didn't have room to set up shop in my apartment. I flagged down a cab, loaded everything into the trunk, and made for Old Town.

Frank was in the office when I got there. I thanked him again for agreeing to help out with Brenda.

"It's a no-brainer," he said. He cast a sidelong glance at my boxes, but said nothing about them.

I took the supplies into the kitchen area and set them up, clamping the press to the table and laying the die and mold out beside them. I needed a heat source. The stove wasn't going to cut it.

"Hey, Frank! We still got that torch around somewhere?" I called down the hallway.

"Think so. Lemme see if I can find it." A few minutes later, he came into the kitchen carrying a little propane cylinder with a torch attachment.

"Perfect," I said.

I spent the next hour melting down the coins I'd bought, pulling the lead bullets out of my ammo, and replacing them with silver ones. Frank hung around watching.

Finally he said, "Think you'll need those?"

I snorted. "Hope not."

It's amazing how much we communicated in those six little words. I knew Frank was asking if I was losing it, if I seriously thought I was going after vampires. My response just as clearly told him that I wasn't sure of much, but that it was better to be prepared for anything. When you've known somebody as long as Frank and I have known each other, you don't need lots of words to say what you mean.

"Okay, then," he said, and ambled back to his office. From down the hallway, I heard him say, "Hope you catch some rabbits."

Before I left, I called Mac to see if he'd found anything on Brenda's computer.

"What do you mean?" he asked. "I found everything—I've got the whole damn system imaged—but I have no idea what any of it means. I know computers, Gray, not real estate."

I rolled my eyes. "All right. You don't have to get snippy. I'll go through it with Brenda later."

I paused at the closet on my way out the door. I looked longingly at my overcoat and fedora, hanging where I'd left them the other day. I was tempted to put them back on, but it wasn't time yet. I still needed to fly under the radar, at least for another day.

21

I made it back to West Town by midafternoon. It was good timing: the lunch rush was over, and the 5 o'clock rush hour hadn't started. I'd planned on snooping around the warehouse, preferably inside, but that might take some doing, depending on the situation.

The first task was to walk the perimeter of the building. It was pretty big, taking up at least half a block. The ground level windows and doors were all boarded up, but the north side of the building was surrounded by chain-link fence covered in green vinyl sheeting with a locked double gate—probably the loading dock, the only working entrance.

I couldn't tell if the building was in use or if it truly was vacant. After that first lap, I knew I couldn't get in any of the doors I'd seen, but if there was one on the loading dock, I might be able to pick its lock. Unlike the cops, I don't need a warrant. Of course, if I was caught, it'd be a breaking and entering charge—trespassing at minimum.

Much like a stakeout, the trick to not getting caught when going somewhere you aren't supposed to go is to look like you're supposed to be wherever you are. It's not about going unseen, it's about going unnoticed. A delivery guy or utility worker is invisible to most people, and they have reason to be just about anywhere. I've been known to wear a uniform when the need arises, but I didn't have the luxury today. Today, it was all about attitude: no casting furtive glances over my shoulder or jumping at unexpected sounds.

Of course, if I was behind an opaque fence, that made the job that much easier. But I didn't want to go in blind; I needed to see what was behind that fence first. If illicit activity was happening here, it stood to reason there'd be guards.

I turned my attention to the buildings across the street,

hoping to find one with a walk-up balcony that would give me an overhead view. Unfortunately, nothing would work.

It was time to get into character.

I walked up to the gate and rattled the chain-link fence.

"Hello," I called, "Anybody in there?"

After a beat, someone called back, "What do you want?" Somebody was home.

"Hey guy, I'm here to pick up a package," I shouted in my best Chicago accent.

After another beat, the voice answered. "We don't know nothing about a package!"

We, huh. So there was more than one guy back there.

"Is this 352 Sangamon? I couldn't find the number anywhere, so I'm running a little late."

"Nah, This is 252," came the answer. "You got the wrong place."

"Aw damn it. Okay, thanks, guy." Then I took off, headed north.

A block down the street, I cut east, then doubled back to the warehouse. I had to find a different way in. Since all the ground-floor entrances were blocked, I turned my gaze upward. The building was three floors high, so there might be an upper window that wasn't boarded up.

Halfway down the building, I saw what I was looking for: a fire escape leading to a door on the third floor. If I could reach the escape ladder, getting in would be a piece of cake.

The bottom rung of the ladder was too high to reach from the ground, so I cast around, looking for something to climb on. The cars parked on the street were too far away. There weren't any conveniently placed trees, nor were there any dumpsters like they show in the movies.

The dumpster idea got me thinking, though. I crossed the street and went down a side alley. Sure enough, there were lines of those heavy-duty plastic trash cans the city distributes for trash collection. Those suckers are tough; one of them should easily hold my 220 pounds.

I wheeled one back to the side of the warehouse and placed it just underneath the fire escape. I scrambled on top, balanced carefully, and grabbed the bottom rung of the ladder. Getting to the next rung was a bit of a struggle, since I couldn't get purchase with my feet yet, but I managed. Then I climbed as quietly as possible, pausing to look in a window on the second floor. It was blacked out, so I couldn't see anything.

At the top, I peered through a window into what looked to be a small storage room; it was empty. Then I turned my attention to the door. It was made of thick metal, with a heavy handle and lock—which was good. Sometimes these emergency doors didn't even have handles and could only be opened from the inside. I took out my lock picks and set to work.

Picking locks takes a lot of practice. The basic concept is pretty simple though: most keyed locks use a set of pins that must line up correctly to allow the barrel of the lock to turn. Without a key, small tools can be used to set each individual pin in place. The part that takes skill is getting each of those pins into the correct position. It requires a feel for tiny movements and tension and friction. I'm not great at it, and I can't pick every lock, but I had this one open in under two minutes. I tried to ease the door open as quietly as possible. I had no idea what was waiting on the other side, and I didn't want to alert anyone to my presence. The door must have been shut for years, though, because it was stuck. I had to put some muscle into it before it came loose with a horrific screech. So much for stealth—

I opted for speed instead.

I jerked hard and the door swung open... revealing an empty hallway.

Okay, back to stealth. I stepped inside and eased the door

shut behind me.

The hallway ran the length of the building. There were doors every ten feet on either side. I crept to the first one, cracked it open and peered inside. It led into the storage room I'd seen through the window. I worked my way down the hallway, carefully checking behind each door. So far, this floor appeared to have been set up as office space for whatever business had occupied the building, though it now sat empty. I finally found a stairwell leading to the lower floors at the end of the hallway.

The flight of stairs went down one floor and ended at a heavy wooden door. This one was in better shape than the outside door, so it didn't take quite as much effort to open, though it did squeak a bit on its hinges. I inched it open a bit at a time until I could get an idea of what was on the other side.

It opened onto an iron catwalk. I couldn't see anything else, because the area was totally dark. I slipped through and crouched on the metal grating, closing the door quickly behind me, then waited for several minutes, letting my eyes adjust and listening for any activity. I could feel the openness of the room: while I still couldn't see anything, I sensed there was no floor beyond the railing. There was a bit of ambient light; eventually my eyes adjusted to a point where I could see a few feet in front of me, but no farther. Hearing nothing, I worked my way along the catwalk, placing my feet lightly so I wouldn't stumble or step on a creaky spot. I passed several places where the walkway branched to the left, away from the wall, over the emptiness of what had to be the main part of the warehouse.

It was strange. There should have been more light in here. My innate sense of distance told me I should have been surrounded by the exterior walls. Even if the windows were boarded up, I should have been able to make out their outlines as sunlight filtered through the cracks, and yet there was nothing. Perhaps the room wasn't as big as I thought, and the main warehouse was partitioned off.

I didn't like the idea of venturing out over open space, so I continued to hug the wall until I came to a metal staircase. I paused before descending to the lower level, and paused once again when I got to the bottom, still listening carefully for any movement. I knew there were at least two men beyond the far wall, and there could very well be others patrolling the interior. The last thing I wanted was to be caught before I found anything.

As I stood there, a shiver went down my spine. Something about this place was giving me the creeps, but I had to keep moving. I shuffled forward a few yards and came to another wall. It was cinderblock, not brick, which confirmed that this area had been partitioned off. I didn't like all this darkness. It was such a big room that I couldn't see anything that was in here. Sure, I could walk the perimeter, or even wander off into the middle, but I'd just be blundering around. I pulled out my phone and debated the risks of using its flashlight app. So little light came in from outside that there was little chance of anyone seeing my own light unless they were in here with me. And if there was someone else in here, they were being very quiet. I'd heard no movement.

I decided to risk it, since I was just as likely to be discovered wandering around blind. I flicked on the light and aimed it toward the center of the room.

LEDs are pretty bright for their size, and in a confined space, like a bedroom or hallway, they work like a charm. In a large, open space like this, however, their light diffuses rather quickly. I held the phone over my head to get the most illumination possible and could just barely make out the far wall. More importantly, though, I spotted low, rectangular blobs at the center of the warehouse. I couldn't make out what they were, but at least they gave me a direction to move in.

I slunk across the floor, more confident in my movements now that I could see where I was going.

When I had covered half the distance, I stopped—froze was more like it. I still couldn't tell what the shapes in front of me were, but a sound had reached my ears. It was a quiet sound, come and gone. I stood deathly still, straining to make sense of it. For a moment there was nothing, and then I caught it again: a low, barely audible breath.

I clicked the light off, plunging myself into darkness once more, and listened.

My own breath crashed into my eardrums, obscuring everything else.

I blocked out my own existence and stretched my senses outward. Sight was useless, so I closed my eyes.

It came again. Breath. Shallow. Slow. Directly ahead.

I took two silent steps forward.

Again, a breath. Wait, no. Two breaths. Two different breaths.

Two more steps. Stop. Listen for a change. No, it stayed the same. Whoever was there was unaware of my presence. Sleeping, maybe? Oh, shit. Rectangular objects in the middle of a darkened room where people were sleeping. My brain conjured images of coffins and dirt and fang-filled jaws.

Stop. Don't panic, investigate. No jumping to conclusions.

I drew my piece and started forward again. Slowly, smoothly, I closed the distance to the source of the sound. I was close now. Very close. Once again, my eyes adjusted to the gloom, and I saw the edge of something just ahead. It wasn't a coffin.

I flicked the light back on and shone it over the scene before me. The rectangular object was definitely not a coffin. It was a cot of some kind, all metal tubing and flimsy mattress-foam, atop of which lay the withered form of a man. Plastic tubes ran in a tangled web from his arms and every orifice to a nearby IV stand holding bags of various sizes and colors. His eyes were closed, and his chest rose and fell in slow, shallow breaths.

I panned the light around to see what else was in the vicinity and found another dozen setups just like this one laid out in neat rows, each supporting a frail, unfortunate soul. As my light washed over the last body, I froze. It was a face I recognized. A face I was supposed to find. Ellie McCarthy lay in a stupor amidst a dozen others, tethered to medical bags for God-knows-what purpose.

22

I quickly strode over to where Ellie lay. She was terribly pale, her cheeks sunken, her eyes ringed with dark circles. I put my ear to her chest. She was breathing, but just barely. Her pulse was weak. I laid a hand on her forehead: it was cool and clammy. I couldn't tell if she was in a coma or just heavily sedated. Despite her pallor, someone appeared to have taken care with her appearance. She was clean, and a blanket had been draped carefully across her naked form.

My first thought was to call 911 and bring the authorities down on this place with a vengeance while I waited by her side. I looked at my phone. Of course, I had no signal in the building. I could go back out the way I'd come and make the call, but now that I'd found her, I couldn't leave her again. Something about this whole situation was abhorrent. I needed to get her out of here. I needed to get them all out of here—but I couldn't do that alone. And right now, Ellie was my priority.

There was no way I could carry Ellie out the way I had come in. That left leaving by the loading dock, and I doubted the fellows I'd spoken with earlier would be too gung-ho about letting that happen.

Before I could move her, though, I had to get her unhooked from all the... stuff that was connected to her.

I turned my attention to the tubes protruding from her limbs and followed each line to its corresponding bag. There were some I recognized, like the saline and glucose, and several I didn't. She also had a catheter and colostomy bag hanging on the side of the bed. After several moments, I decided I could unhook everything safely. I wasn't sure what effect that would have, whether she would wake up soon after being disconnected from the mysterious chemicals coursing through her system or if it would send her into some sort of shock, but I had to take the chance. Leaving her here simply wasn't an option.

I re-holstered the .45 and set about carefully removing everything. Once all the tubing was clear, I wrapped the blanket around her and lifted her gently in my arms. She was so thin, it felt like I was lifting a child. Though her weight wouldn't impede me, I needed a free hand, so I shifted her onto my left shoulder in a fireman's carry, then held my phone aloft to illuminate the surroundings.

I spotted a door on the east wall and made a beeline for it. Once I reached the door, I pocketed the phone and drew the .45, settling its weight in my grip. I worked the handle with my foot and pulled the door open. Light flooded in.

The hallway we were in ran the length of the building. I knew the loading dock was on the north side, so I headed that way. We came to a corner and I stopped. I couldn't put my back to the wall like I normally would, so I had to be satisfied with inching forward until I could see down the corridor and hope I wouldn't expose myself.

Halfway down, I saw a big roll-up style garage door next to a smaller metal exit. My brain was scrambling to come up with a plan to get us out of here as quickly as possible. Carrying Ellie, I wasn't in the best position to fight my way out, but my trigger finger worked just fine. I didn't want to shoot anyone, per se, but whatever was going on in here definitely qualified as creepy, which placed the goons guarding this mess into the lowlife category. If lead started flying, I wouldn't lose much sleep over it.

A half-assed idea popped into my head. It wasn't the most solid plan I'd ever come up with, and there were no guarantees it would work, but it gave me the element of surprise and could potentially take out one of the guys pretty quick. There were at least two on the other side of the door, maybe more. I didn't know what else to do, so I went with it.

I stood directly in front of the exit, then leaned as far toward the roll-up as I could and banged on it twice with the butt of my pistol. Then I straightened up and waited.

Muffled voices came from outside. I couldn't tell what they said, but I didn't care. I was watching the door very closely. The latch lifted, and the door began to open.

The second I was certain the latch had cleared the door frame, I slammed my right foot into the center of the door with as much force as I could muster. The door flew backward, sending the guy who was opening it sprawling off the loading dock onto the concrete below.

I stepped onto the dock, pistol barrel leading the way, and swung to the left. A heavyset guy with a tattooed bald head, caught off guard by my sudden appearance, was fumbling with his own gun in the waistband of his jeans. I aimed mine at the spot right between his eyes and said, "Don't." The guy froze.

"Use two fingers and toss the gun," I told him.

Slowly, he did. The 9mm Beretta clattered onto the pavement below.

"Turn around." He did.

I glanced at the other guy lying a few feet away. He was moaning and groaning, but wasn't trying to get back to his feet yet.

"Keys to the gate?" I asked the one still standing.

"In my pocket."

"With one hand, I want you to take them out very slowly. I see anything other than keys come out of that pocket, I shoot you and find them myself. Understood?"

He mumbled an affirmative and did so. Then I directed him over to the gate, giving his buddy a wide berth, and had him unlock it. He kept muttering to himself about how "they" were going to kill him. His eyes just about bugged out of his head when I had him toss the keys into the road, then lock himself back inside once I had Ellie safely out.

I put the pistol away, then shifted Ellie back to both arms and ran for the closest intersection, where I hailed a cab to Rush Medical Center.

23

On the way to the hospital, with Ellie's head cradled gently in my lap, I phoned Alderman Juarez and told him that I'd located his fiancée and where we were headed. Then I called her father and told him the same. Next, I called Jack Larsen.

Jack seemed hesitant to talk to me at first. He said Detective Rowe had been breathing down his neck ever since he'd visited me in the hospital. So I told him all about the warehouse and what I'd found there. He let out a low whistle when I finished the story.

"I'll get someone over there as soon as I can, but it'll take a while. You know how these things work. And don't be surprised to get another visit from Rowe."

"Right," I said. "There's something else. This warehouse belongs to a real estate company that may be involved in the whole thing. I've got a bunch of data to sift through, but in light of what I found, maybe I should turn it all over to you guys."

"Not a bad idea. Might get Rowe off your back for a while."

I mulled that over. Even though I could officially close this case, I had a niggling thought that it wasn't over yet. Something told me I'd been skirting around the edges of something big—I'd smelled the storm brewing for a while. My guess was that rescuing Ellie had put me right in the center of it. It couldn't hurt to throw the detective a bone, to give him something to gnaw on for a while instead of dogging my every move. Yeah, it wasn't a bad idea to share the data.

I told Jack I'd be in touch, and if he needed anything more from me, I'd be at the hospital.

***

The sun quickly lost its grasp on the sky, and the fiery colors of sunset gave way to twilight as we reached the ER. The doctors and nurses hesitated to start treatment on Ellie until I informed them that her father was on the way, as well as Alderman Juarez, who had a special interest in her condition. They had lots of questions about what had happened to her, which I answered as best I could. They were particularly interested in what types of pharmaceuticals she had received. Unfortunately, I couldn't provide much help there.

After the initial flurry of activity and barrage of questions during the admission process, things quieted. The hospital staff were waiting on lab results and a transfer to a room upstairs. I sat in the chair next to Elllie's bed for an hour, trying to figure out what the hell had been going on at the warehouse. Why were all those people being kept there like that? It wasn't what I had expected from slave traders. The setup seemed too permanent. I could understand keeping them sedated, but all the rest didn't make sense. My train of thought was interrupted when Mr. McCarthy arrived. He thanked me profusely for finding his daughter and asked a few questions about her condition. I didn't really know, so all I could do was assure him that the doctors were doing what they could. He didn't ask where I'd found her or what had happened to her. That seemed odd to me, so I asked him if he wanted to know.

A shadow passed over his face, and then he answered. "No. All that matters is that she's here now. Whatever happened, it can't be good, but it's in the past. Knowing about it would only cause me more heartache, and I've had all of that I can take."

I nodded. That approach to life must be nice, truly living in the present. I couldn't do it. I always needed explanations, reasons, answers. It's what drove me. It's why, even though my job was finished here, I'd keep digging. I needed to know.

Just then, Juarez calmly stepped through the curtain and absorbed the scene before him. Before the curtain closed, I caught a glimpse of his bodyguard, the same one from the pub, standing just on the other side. After a beat, Juarez met my eyes and nodded slightly, then turned his attention to the old man kneeling beside the bed.

"Mr. McCarthy, my name is Arthur. I'm a friend of Ellie's." There was a tightness in his voice, and I could tell he was making an effort to keep it together. I decided to give them some privacy, so I excused myself, slipped through the curtain, and found my way outside for a smoke.

24

Ryley stirred. His wounds were healing quickly, though not as quickly as he would have liked. It was his pride, more than anything, that had been injured. The others had given him looks that would freeze hellfire since he'd stumbled back to headquarters with a belly full of lead.

He had failed, and everyone knew it. The master should have ended it then and there—such were the expected consequences. But instead he had been demoted, which was proving to be an even worse punishment. This was the fourth night since the debacle, and while his body was functional again, his confidence would take something more than mere time to recover. He needed to get back into everyone's good graces, but all he could think about was revenge.

Just then, he heard a commotion outside his room: raised voices and lots of movement. He pulled on a pair of jeans, stuck his head out the door, and grabbed a familiar as he raced past. At least Ryley still outranked them.

"What's happening?" he asked.

"The warehouse has been compromised," the kid said. "We're meeting in the commons to get our orders now." He scurried off down the hall.

Ryley snatched a shirt from the back of a chair and pulled it over his head, hiding the pink, puckered scars of his wounds, then he, too, raced for the commons.

"...don't know how long we've got, so we're moving them now!" the Sire called to the small group that had gathered. "You all know the protocol and have your assignments. We've planned for this possibility. No more mistakes. Now get going!"

The others dispersed, moving with a clarity of purpose. The shit was in the fan, and they all wanted to do their best to avoid the mess. As the crowd cleared, the Sire's eyes, smoldering with anger, found Ryley's. He crooked a finger at Ryley, then turned and strode toward a door at the far side of the room. Ryley fell in behind him.

They walked through a short corridor and down a flight of stairs, stopping before a small alcove cut into the concrete walls and sealed off with iron bars. Inside sat two men. One was busted up pretty badly and seemed to be in a daze. The other, a large man with a tattooed head, had wild, darting eyes. The fear rolled off him in waves. Ryley's stomach lurched, it was so pungent.

"These men failed to protect the warehouse," his master said. "They've been forthcoming about what happened. Make sure they haven't left anything out."

***

Twenty minutes later, Ryley emerged from the cell, confident that the two familiars had told him the whole story. It was unfortunate that one of them had died during the interrogation. That would have to stay quiet if recruitment were to continue. Couldn't build a bad reputation among the rabble of the city.

Ryley reported immediately, humbling himself before Elijah. "It was him. The detective." Ryley had a hard time not choking on the word. "Their description fits."

"Wonderful," hissed Elijah.

Ryley could feel the rage building around him. This was his fault. If he hadn't botched the hit, this never would have happened. He needed to make amends now, or he might not survive the next five minutes.

"Sir," he began. "I know this can't be fixed at the moment, but if revenge would be a suitable alternative, I have an idea."

Elijah's eyes flashed dangerously.

"Tell me."

So he did.

25

Outside the hospital, I'd retrieved what passed for coffee from a vending machine and was halfway through another cigarette when I heard footsteps behind me. I glanced over my shoulder. It was Juarez.

"Thank you," he said.

"What's the prognosis?" I asked between drags.

"It's unclear at this time. She's still unconscious, but the doctors are confident she'll come around."

"Good. That's good."

There was a brief pause.

"I'm afraid to ask, but I need to know. Where did you find her?"

"In a warehouse in West Town. She was being held, sedated. You were on to something with the human trafficking thing, but I think there's more to it than that." I intentionally left out the working theory I'd developed over my first smoke. It involved vampires and regular bloodletting. It fit with everything I'd learned the last few days, but I didn't think Juarez would take it well.

"Any idea who was behind it?"

"Maybe." I took another drag. "I've got a line on some intel from the management company that owns the warehouse. Nothing solid yet, but I'll keep you in the loop."

Juarez nodded. "I'd appreciate that." He offered his hand, and I shook it. "Thank you again." He turned and walked back into the hospital, no doubt to wait by Ellie's side until she woke.

I sighed. That kind of love seemed so foreign to me. I'd had my share of relationships, though nothing recently, and one or two had gotten pretty serious, but I'd never felt a connection like the one Juarez seemed to have with Ellie. I envied them. Maybe one day I'd be lucky enough to experience something like that.

I dropped the cigarette, crushed it, and made my way to the closest bus stop. I debated going to the hotel to check on Brenda, but I was tired and needed a good night's sleep. The question was, did I make the trek all the way back home, or did I crash at the office? The office was pretty appealing. I made a mental map of the quickest route and then stood there. Waiting.

That's the biggest problem with public transportation: the waiting. Normally, it doesn't bother me much. I read a lot. I daydream. I ponder the meaning of the universe. But sometimes it gets really tedious, like now. I wanted nothing more than to roll up in front of the building within a matter of minutes, let myself in, and pass out with my face scrunched into a couch cushion. Sure, I could hail a cab, but they were expensive. I wasn't on a schedule at the moment, so there was no reason not to take the bus.

I checked my phone. No new messages or emails. I Googled vampires for the hell of it and found lots of urban fantasy and romance novels. Finally, the bus pulled up, and I climbed aboard. Two transfers and thirty minutes later, I reached the office, let myself in, and flopped onto the couch.

It seemed like only minutes had gone by when my phone rang. I seriously considered flinging it against the wall, but changed my mind at the last second. Instead, I checked the caller ID: it was Frank. I thumbed the phone on and mumbled something. Probably hello.

Frank's ragged voice filled my ear. "Stay where you are," he croaked. "Don't play their game."

I sat up, fully awake now.

"Frank, what's going on?"

A silky voice with a British accent spoke next. "Mr. Gray, you've been a thorn in my side for long enough. If you wish to see your partner alive again, I strongly suggest you meet me in the Grand Ballroom at Navy Pier... alone. You have one hour. If you do not arrive within that time, Frank will be dead, and you will receive another phone call from his wife. Do I make myself clear?" I knew that voice. I couldn't place it, but it was familiar.

"Crystal," I growled through clenched teeth, on my feet now. "Let *me* make something clear, you limey bastard. If anything happens to Frank, you better kill me when I get there, because I won't stop until I take you apart." Crimson clouded the edge of my vision.

"I am a man of my word, Mr. Gray. Don't ever doubt that."

The line went dead.

I tried calling back, but it went straight to voicemail.

Son of a bitch. They had Frank, whoever they were. I had no doubt that if I didn't show up, they'd kill him and then go after his family. I clenched my fists... and felt the phone crunch in my grip. Looking down, I saw that it was shattered. Shit. That wasn't good. Or normal. I needed to calm down. I needed to think. I had to go—I couldn't let anything happen to Frank or his family—but going alone was insane. It was clearly a setup. I would likely be outnumbered and outgunned. If these people really were vampires, or something, and had the strength and speed of the last one I'd run into, they'd turn me into meat paste. I needed a plan.

I sat on the edge of the couch and thought. Okay, cover your ass, Gray. First, make sure Nancy and the kids are okay. I'd just hulk-smashed my phone to death, so I picked up the landline on my desk and dialed their number. It rang seven times before the answering machine picked up. I glanced at my watch: one o'clock in the morning. Hopefully, Nancy was asleep and not kidnapped or worse.

"Nancy, if you're there, pick up the phone! It's Earl." She was the only one who got to call me that. I waited a few seconds, then hung up and dialed again. This time, she picked up on the fourth ring.

"Nancy, are you okay?"

"I'm fine, Earl. What in heaven's name is going on? Is something wrong with Frank?" Her volume rose with her fear. Scaring her like this felt like a knife twisting in my chest.

"I'm sorry Nancy. I don't have time to explain everything right now, but I think you and the kids may be in danger. I need you to gather them up and get out of the house. Take the car, and go to the police station. Stay there until Frank or I come to get you. Understand?"

"You're scaring me, Earl," she said, her voice wavering.

"I know, and I'm sorry. This is important. Can you do it?"

"Yes," she whispered. I could hear her tears starting to fall.

"Good. I'll talk to you soon," I said, trying to stay positive. I truly hoped it would be Frank coming to get them.

I needed backup. I wanted to call in the cavalry and swoop down on these assholes, raining death and mayhem upon them like a hurricane for threatening the closest thing to family I had.

But there was no backup. The cops were already stretched thin, and I wasn't sure I could trust them, anyway. Calling them in could turn out to be just a couple of more guns pointed my way. Plus, Rowe was convinced I was a murderer, so I really didn't want him around if I did end up killing a few folks tonight. Mac also wasn't an option. What would he do, ping them to death? That assassin, Harrison, would be nice to have in my corner right about now. I wondered if he'd be willing to help out a former mark. Not that it mattered; it's not like he'd left a business card. I had no idea how to get in contact with him. No, it looked like I was on my own for this. Unless...

What was it Harrison had said? *Are you a reader? I am. So many connections can be made that way.* The man spoke in riddles, could this have been one of them? Was he referring to a missed-connection classified page? There used to be a section in the Chicago Reader, but Craigslist had replaced it. Well, it couldn't hurt to give it a shot.

I booted up my office computer and went to the appropriate page. It only took a minute or two to write what I wanted, something that I hoped would catch his eye: *Harrison—going fishing at Navy Pier. Could use a good netter. Gray.* I had no idea if he'd get the message, but I had nothing to lose.

I got up, checked that my .45 was loaded and that I had a spare mag—I might just get to try out my new handloads—and retrieved my trenchcoat from the closet. There was no point in hiding anymore. If I was going out, I was going out in style. Well, my style, anyway.

26

Most people know Navy Pier as a giant tourist attraction, which it is, with lots of overpriced entertainments and souvenir shops, which it has. Its iconic Ferris wheel looms overhead, inducing vertigo even in those with feet firmly planted on the ground. Less well known are the structures and locations farther out on the pier, such as the beer garden and, my destination, the Aon Grand Ballroom.

At night, the pier is off limits: the walkways are gated and the buildings locked up tight. You can still go down there if you want—Grand Avenue runs almost the entire length of the pier—but after hours, there's nothing to see.

I had the cab drop me off about three quarters of the way down. It was still a short walk to the ballroom, but I didn't want to give away my arrival by pulling directly up to the entrance. I got out, gave him a nice tip with a note saying to call 911 wrapped up in it, and told him to leave. Hopefully, he wouldn't see it for a while.

A light breeze blew off the lake. The water-purification plant next door hummed at its never-ending work. A multi-level parking garage obscured most of the skyscrapers from my sight. There were several streetlights spaced along the road, and a few pleasure craft twinkled out on the lake, but for the most part, it was dark.

There are few truly quiet places in a town as big as Chicago, but at two o'clock in the morning, this was one of them. A place that's usually alive and vibrating with the energy of tens of thousands of people during the day is super creepy when it's completely deserted.

By my watch, I still had twenty minutes before the hour was up, which gave me a few minutes to scope things out, but not nearly enough time for a thorough recon.

I hurried down the sidewalk beneath the newly-installed windows of the ballroom. I'd have loved to take a peek inside and get a feel for what awaited me, but they were eighty feet up with no easy access.

The Grand Ballroom was an excellent place for an ambush. Though there were multiple entrances on three different levels, all of them funneled down to two points on the ground floor before entering the ballroom proper. It would be easy to let me slip inside, then seal off the exits. Even so, I didn't like the idea of waltzing in by the first open door I came to.

Even though I couldn't get up to the new windows, the second floor had a wrap-around enclosed balcony that could give me a sneak peek, assuming I could get up there without drawing attention.

I ducked into a service entrance bay. All of the exterior doors would be locked up for the night, but I was pretty sure I could get past one of them. I quickly found the entrance closest to the stairs and, after a few minutes, let myself inside. This lock was easier to work than the one at the warehouse: it was used a lot more, and it didn't stick.

Once inside, I listened for movement, for any sign that I had been detected. Hearing nothing, I ran up the stairwell to the second floor, the Festival Hall, a giant exhibit hall used for conventions and the like. I poked my head into a long corridor that ran the length of the hall. I didn't see or hear any patrols, so I stepped out and took a left toward the Lakeview Terrace. Brick pillars supported this stretch of building that connected the exhibit hall to the ballroom. It was set up for a function, with a bunch of tables covered in white linen lined up neatly in the center. I wove my way between them to the wall of glass doors that led to the upper ballroom lobby.

I crouched low as I approached, minimizing my bulk, then peered through the windows. The lobby looked empty. A pair of bathrooms were set into the far wall. The safety lights above them had a minimal glow, casting shadows on the carpeted floor below. I waited a moment longer, then saw a flash of movement. Sure enough, a lone figure was half-hidden behind a brick pillar. He didn't look to be on high alert, but was casually scanning the lobby. As he swung his head to the left, I saw some sort of apparatus strapped to his head—night vision, maybe? Then he shifted on his feet, and the tip of an MP something-or-other swung into view. Despite my fondness for sidearms, I'm not really a gun expert; all I could tell was that it was a compact submachine gun of some kind.

Huh. Night vision and firepower didn't scream vampire to me. Regular humans, I knew how to deal with.

I drew my .45 and held it at my chest, glancing at my watch as I did so. Only ten minutes left. Damn it, I was cutting this close.

There was no way I was getting through the door without drawing the hired goon's attention. If I did, the game was over. I also didn't want to shoot him right here; that would no doubt draw the attention of everyone else in the building. Also game over. I needed him to come to me.

I crawled back to the closest table, keeping as low a profile as possible. The henchman wasn't looking in my direction at the moment, but there was no sense in being careless. I grabbed a spoon off the table, then crawled back and crouched behind a pillar. I chucked the spoon at one of the doors kitty-corner from me—not hard enough to break anything, just enough to make a noise.

The hireling whipped around, gun leading the way. He honed right in on the spot the spoon had hit, then approached the doors, sweeping his goggles left and right.

Come on out, I thought. You know you want to investigate. He stood there for a tense thirty seconds, scouring the darkness for the source of the mysterious sound. Then he turned and walked back to his spot by the pillar, though he kept glancing back over his shoulder.

Crap.

I didn't want to risk crawling across open space now that he was paying attention, so no more spoons. I should have thought to grab a few. What to use now?

I pulled the spare magazine from my pocket and thumbed out a shell. I didn't like wasting ammo, but if it got the job done, it was worth it. I lobbed the shell at the glass. It made a satisfying clack: not as solid as the spoon, but good enough. This time, the guard hustled over to the sound and walked the length of the doors. Seeing nothing, he pushed one open and stepped onto the terrace with me, leaving one foot propped against the door.

I had to time this perfectly; otherwise, I'd get shot. I waited until he angled his body to his left, away from me, then slipped around my pillar and leapt to him. He sensed me coming and swung back to get a bead on me, but I was too close. With my right hand, I slammed my knuckles into his Adam's apple to cut off his windpipe, so he couldn't shout for help. Then I crunched his left knee. As he dropped, I finished him off with a left cross.

I had no way to tie him up, so I just had to hope he'd stay night-night long enough for me to do what I needed. I stripped the mag and chambered round from his automatic and stuffed them in my coat pocket, then slid the rifle across the floor and under a table. I yanked the night-vision goggles off his head and strapped them onto my own. While I was doing that, I noticed he had a radio connected to an earpiece, and took that too. I figured it might be good to listen in on enemy chatter.

Once I had everything on and adjusted, I stepped into the lobby and crept to the balcony entrance. I didn't need to go far: the first window was about ten feet in. I sidled up next to it and tried to peer down into the ballroom. I wasn't used to night-vision, and my brain was having a hard time interpreting what I was seeing, plus the goggles were uncomfortable and awkward to wear. I decided I was better off without them, so I stripped them off and placed them on the floor. It was pretty dark, but there was a little light coming from somewhere—probably bulbs above that never turned off completely for safety reasons.

In the center of the room was a man strapped to a metal folding chair. I couldn't make out any details, but I assumed it was Frank. Several other figures paced around the center of the room. They didn't appear to be armed.

I turned my attention to the rest of the balcony and scanned the windows, checking if any other cronies were covering things from the higher vantage point. I didn't see anything, but that didn't mean they weren't there.

I didn't like this setup at all. There was no way I could get to Frank without completely exposing myself. I wanted another half an hour to clear the balcony before going out there, but my time was almost up.

As if on cue, a voice began to speak, resonating through the chamber below. It was loud enough that I could easily hear it through the glass. "Mr. Gray, if you are hiding somewhere in the shadows, you have precisely two minutes to show yourself." I finally placed the voice: the Brit from the nightclub who'd sworn he knew nothing about Ellie.

I had to choose: call his bluff and wait for an opportunity to present itself, or offer myself up and hope for the best. Something told me he wasn't bluffing, so I made the only choice I could.

I backed out of the balcony and walked down the stairs. In my head I heard the whistle from *The Good, the Bad and the Ugly*. I might die tonight, but I wasn't going without a fight.

27

The Aon Grand Ballroom is huge: 18,000 square feet of tiled floor beneath a soaring domed ceiling that reaches eighty feet at its apex. The east wall is filled with windows overlooking Lake Michigan.

I walked through the entryway and immediately felt dwarfed by the cavernous space. Frank was out there in the middle; the distance between us seemed to stretch out forever. If Fangs decided to do something, I'd never be able to reach him in time.

As I strode passed the stage on my left, I announced, "Don't get your knickers in a bunch. I'm here." Maybe not the wittiest thing to say, but that's what came out.

Eli stood halfway between Frank and the east wall, facing away from me, hands clasped behind his back. His blond, spiky hair was unmistakable. He turned at the sound of my voice, and a depraved smile tugged at the corners of his mouth.

I blinked, and suddenly he was standing directly behind Frank. I froze. I hadn't even seen him move. Holy shit.

He grabbed Frank by the hair and tilted his head up.

"See," he said, "I told you he would come. Friendship above all ties does bind the heart."

"Go to hell," Frank croaked. He sounded awful. Now that my eyes had adjusted, I saw the bruises on his face, his bloodied nose.

Eli laughed, and I started forward again. I'd gone five steps when the laughter stopped abruptly, and he glared at me. "That's far enough Mr. Gray."

A voice crackled in my ear, "The exits are sealed." A minion reporting over the comm.

I glanced over my shoulder and saw a silhouette in the archway behind me. When I looked back to Eli, there was another man standing beside him. I use the term "man" loosely—he looked more like a punk teenager—but I recognized him too. It was the maniac who had attacked me, the one I'd emptied an entire magazine into. This just kept getting better.

The skeptical part of my brain let out a death rattle as the credulous part jumped up and down screaming, *See! See! Vampires are real! It must have been written all over my face.*

"I see you remember Ryley," Eli commented. "My associate has found himself in a bit of a pickle. You see, I am not fond of failure, and it is his failure that has brought us to this unfortunate crossroad. However, he devised this scheme to draw you out in an attempt to redeem himself. Full redemption, of course, can only be earned once he completes his original assignment." He turned to Ryley and gestured at me. "If you will."

Ryley smiled evilly and answered, "Of course."

It was all the warning I got. I'd tangled with this punk already, and I knew how fast he was. His speed paled in comparison to Eli's, as I'd just witnessed, but he was far faster than any normal human. Of course, he had a much greater distance to travel than my arm did.

I swung the .45 up as he came across the floor. I'd never have time to track him, so I aimed for the point where he and the bullet would meet, about three feet in front of me. As soon as my arm completed its arc, I pulled the trigger. The explosion echoed off the domed ceiling in a deafening roar, and I stepped to the side.

The vampire's momentum carried him right through the space I had previously occupied. He crumpled to the floor and slid across the tile. My aim had been true, and the bullet had buried itself in his brain. He didn't even twitch. I guess the silver worked.

I turned back to Eli, who appeared confused, and leveled the gun at him.

"Silver," I said, "Who knew?"

Eli recovered quickly and spouted another quote. "For he, indeed, who looks into the face of a friend beholds, as it were, a copy of himself." Quick as a thought, he grabbed Frank's head in both hands and twisted, vertebrae popping, severing his spinal cord.

A bestial roar erupted from my chest. "No!" I screamed as I fired again and again. But Eli was much faster than Ryley, and I missed every shot. By the time I had emptied the magazine, hot tears of hatred and anguish were streaming down my face.

Eli appeared at Frank's side and looked at me with irritation. "Your turn," he spat.

I released the spent mag and slammed the spare in.

The comm crackled again, and I heard, "Take him."

I had just enough presence of mind to drop to the floor as the muffled cracks of silenced gunfire broke out behind me. I scrambled backward, hoping to put my back to the stage and frustrate the minions in the doorways with an impossible angle to hit me. Amazingly, I made it. Glass shattered above me. I looked up to see movement in the balcony above. More minions. I threw my hands over my head—I don't know why; they wouldn't stop bullets. It was pure instinct. A couple of rounds thunkd into the tile around me. More glass broke. What a crappy way to go out. Oh well, at least I'd taken one of them with me.

The comm crackled again, and there was some confused shouting, but I was so scared I couldn't make sense of it. A second or two passed, and I wasn't dead. Weird. In fact, I hadn't heard any more gunshots. I lowered my hands and saw Eli in the same spot, glaring at me. His eyes were burning: seriously, they were glowing red. That couldn't be good.

I glanced at the balcony, but didn't see anything. Maybe they had repositioned? I didn't have time to dwell on it, though, because Eli's voice cut through my surprise. "Fine, I'll do it myself."

He blurred, closing the distance between us in half a heartbeat, and reached for me with those well-manicured hands. The next thing I knew, I was flying through the air. I hit the floor hard and slid into something. Frank. He was still strapped to the chair, his body hanging limp like a rag doll. Seeing him like that, the man who had saved me from myself, the man who I had been unable to save from this savage, tore at my very soul. Anger welled up deep inside me, and I felt something break. I don't know what; my sanity, maybe.

Rivers of red sprang into existence around me: not blood, but the pulsing energy I'd seen in my dreams. I placed my hands into the stream swirling beside me and felt my anger double. I pushed myself off the floor and turned to face Eli, who was rushing me again.

My eyes told me he was still moving with the same speed, but my brain said, *So what? You know where he'll be*. With that thought, he seemed to slow to almost normal. When he lunged for me again, I lashed out, throwing all my weight into a right hook. My fist met his nose with a meaty crunch, and his head snapped back. He didn't fall, but spun around and stopped, blood pouring from his nose. His eyes went wide, and his mouth opened as if to say something, but I didn't let him. I followed up with a left cross that staggered him. A tooth skittered across the floor.

He jumped out of reach, narrowed his eyes, and squared off.

Somewhere in the far reaches of my brain, common sense was trying to tell me that going head to head with this monster was a bad idea, that there were still goons with automatic weapons somewhere on the periphery, that none of what was happening made any sense. It didn't matter. The pissed-off monster inside me was in control, and when did he ever listen to common sense?

Eli rushed me yet again, hissing between pointy teeth. He reached for me, and I batted his hand away, but he spun with the redirection and threw an elbow at my face. I barely got my hand up in time to block it, but it still knocked me off balance. He took the opportunity to land a solid kick on my outer thigh. The power behind that kick was immense. It should have snapped my femur in half, but it didn't, though it hurt like hell.

He tackled me then, and we both hit the floor, grappling for the upper hand. He bared his teeth and lunged for my throat. I threw an arm up, and he latched onto it instead, biting down hard. I screamed and punched him in the side of the head with my free hand.

I couldn't keep this up. Even with the boost of strength I'd somehow managed, he was still winning. I needed my gun if I was going to put him down for good, but it was still lying over by the stage, where I'd dropped it when he'd flung me across the room.

Another punch to the head, and his teeth ripped free of my flesh. I gouged him in the eye and pushed him off to the side, then scrambled to my feet. He did the same. We were back to square one, except now blood was streaming from my arm, and it looked like his broken nose was healing already.

Fight smart and fight dirty, I told myself. Don't play by his rules.

We circled each other. I tried to position myself in line with the gun, but with him in between. Once I was where I needed to be, I presented an opening. A trained fighter would have recognized it for what it was and ignored it or feigned an attack to make an actual opening.

Eli wasn't a trained fighter. He took the bait and lunged.

Rather than bat him aside like I'd done before, I stepped into the attack, grabbed his arm, and executed a flawless jiu-jitsu hip throw. Once he was on the ground, I put him in a shoulder arm-lock, pinning his head to the floor with my knee. Then came the dirty part. I used the leverage to yank his arm straight up, popping his shoulder out of socket. He yelped in pain. Good. I hopped to my feet and kicked him in the back of the head as hard as I could, for good measure, then sprinted for the gun.

I almost made it.

I was only a few feet away when Eli hit me from behind. His high tackle knocked me down and put him in an excellent position to mount an offensive. I twisted around so I could get my arms up to defend myself, but he had my hips pinned. No matter how hard I struggled, I couldn't get free. He rained down blows hard and fast, one after another. I felt like Scott Farkus from *A Christmas Story* as Ralphie beat the snot out of him.

I fended off the worst of the blows, but my strength was waning; I had lost a lot of blood from the gash on my arm and I was fading fast. I kept my good arm up and flailed with my wounded arm trying to reach the gun, but it was a few inches beyond my fingertips. I guess it was meat paste time for me. Well, I'd made a good show of things at least.

A shadow fell across me, looming over us. Eli didn't notice, so I assumed it was Death here to take me away. He looked strange, dressed in black fatigues and ski mask, sporting a rifle with a giant scope instead of a scythe. A heavy blow landed, and I felt my jaw break.

Death moved his foot, like he was kicking something.

Cold iron touched my fingers. My pistol? Yes.

I closed my hand around the grip and, with the last of my strength, pointed it at Eli and pulled the trigger.

The silver slug ripped through his face and out the back of his skull, sending a spray of blood, bone fragments, and gray matter into the air. He slumped forward on top of me.

I looked up, but Death wasn't there, so I stared at the ceiling until everything went black.

28

When I woke up, I was in the hospital. Again. I tried to open my eyes, but couldn't; they were swollen shut. Not surprising, considering the beating I'd taken. At least I was alive—that was good.

Then I remembered Frank. He was dead, and it was my fault. I hadn't been fast enough or smart enough to save him. I was the one who had gotten involved in this nightmare, not him. I didn't deserve to be alive. My thoughts spiraled into a dark whirlpool of depression. I lay there with them for a while before drifting back into oblivion.

***

I played with the pretty blue lights for a time. They made me happy, helped me forget the darkness for a while. The red ones were there too, but I wanted no part of them.

***

The next time I woke up, I could see. Sunlight beamed through the window beside the hospital bed. I wanted it to go away. I wanted it to be dark again. I lay there for a while, watching the dust motes dance in the beams of light.

Finally, I heard rustling on my other side, so I turned to the nurse who was changing my IV bag. She was pretty. She glanced at me and gave a little start, like she was surprised to find me watching her.

"Oh! You're awake!"

"Nope. I'm sleeping with my eyes open," was what I tried to say. Except my jaw wouldn't move; all that I got out was, "Nmph."

Oh right. Broken jaw. Probably wired shut. Funny, it didn't hurt that much.

The pretty nurse rushed off to get a doctor. What followed was a long line of specialists parading through my room to marvel at my recovery. Apparently, it was a miracle that I'd survived at all, given the injuries I had sustained, but even more miraculous was how fast I was healing. I'd been out for two days, but most of the doctors hadn't been sure I'd ever wake up. I'd suffered a pretty bad concussion—I guess getting your head pounded repeatedly by a hacked-off vampire will do that to a guy.

New X-rays showed that my jaw was mending extraordinarily fast, so fast they worried I might heal over the wire, so they took it out. The swelling had all but disappeared, and the gash on my arm was already scabbing over.

The doctors were full of questions about my diet and what supplements I was taking. All I said was, "I drink a lot of gin." I didn't have a good answer for them, anyway. Not one they would believe. "Yeah, I play with these strange blue lights when I'm dreaming, and presto, I heal faster." That would probably get me committed.

Even though I was healing quickly, the doctors wanted to keep me for observation for a couple of days.

Once I could talk, Detective Rowe came by with a bunch of questions. Mac had turned over all the data from Brenda's computer, and the forensic guys had found all kinds of evidence of real estate fraud. It wasn't my area of expertise, so I glazed over at all the details.

This time I told him everything. Well, not everything, but about the McCarthy case and the human trafficking ring and how that had led me to Brenda and the warehouse and finding Ellie. I told him about the phone call and Frank's kidnapping and my desperate attempt to save him. I might have broken down a bit when I got to that part.

Rowe told me that nothing had been found at the warehouse, but Ellie had woken up and reported that she had, in fact, been kidnapped, though she had no idea where she was held. Due to the sedation, she couldn't remember anything about her captivity. He still seemed a little miffed about being kept in the dark for so long, but Alderman Juarez had come to my defense, telling him that he had requested complete confidentiality while I was working the case. Rowe didn't say much about the fiasco at the pier, but I could tell he was somewhat sympathetic concerning Frank. After everything came out, the pieces fit together so nicely that no charges were filed against me. I guess it was good having friends in high places.

Not that I really cared. I was still in a pretty bad headspace.

Mac came by as well. He didn't ask as many questions, but he talked nonstop for an hour. The incident at the pier had made the papers, he said. The cab driver had indeed found my note and called 911. By the time the responders arrived, no one was moving inside. They had found eight bodies, including mine. Six of them had been shot. That was strange: I could account for two of them, Ryley and Eli, but who had killed the other four? Had they shot each other by mistake?

When I told Mac my phone had been smashed to smithereens, he went right out and bought me a brand new one, despite my protests. He said it was my "I'm glad you're not dead" present. At least that made one of us.

He showed me all the new features, downloaded some of his favorite apps, and even put a couple of personalized ringtones on it for me. He thought the Law and Order "thunk thunk" was particularly clever; he said it was ironic that it had taken someone who had been kicked off the force to actually bring some law and order back to this town. Is that what I had done? I wasn't so sure.

"Oh, yeah, in case you were wondering," he said, "I found the source of the spyware that infected your computer. It came from that real estate place. I figured since it was in the vicinity of the IP address, I'd take a look."

"Brenda's computer?" I asked.

"No, a different terminal."

That made sense. The owners of the warehouse were clearly in league with the kidnappers, if not one and the same. Deleting the files from my computer would have kept anyone investigating my murder from looking into Ellie's disappearance and dragging them out from the shadows. Guess that hadn't worked out for them.

I wondered how Brenda was doing and thought about calling her, but I fell asleep before I got around to it.

***

Later that night there was a soft knock on the door. My breath caught. I could tell exactly who was here. The almost non-existent shooshing sound a coat makes when rubbing against a super-soft sweater and the faint whiff of fabric softener and jasmine that wafted into the room gave her away. I wasn't ready for this. Not yet. I closed my eyes and pretended to be asleep.

She sat down next to me and placed her hand ever so gently on my arm.

"I know you're awake, Gray," she said quietly.

I opened my eyes and looked at her graying hair, at the small wrinkles around her eyes that spoke of a lifetime of joy. It was too much. Tears leaked from my eyes and rolled down my cheeks.

"I'm sorry, Nancy. I'm so sorry."

She patted my arm tenderly. "It wasn't your fault."

"I failed him. When he needed me most, I failed." I choked back a sob.

"No," she said. "When he needed you most, you were there. You showed up. You fought for him." Now she was crying too. "Good Lord, look at you. Look at how hard you fought. That's more than anyone could hope for."

"It wasn't enough."

"What would have happened if you hadn't shown up?"

"They would have killed him and then come after you and the kids," I whispered.

"But you stopped them. We're safe because of you." She took a deep, shuddering breath. "This is a terrible loss, and our lives will never be the same, but you didn't fail us."

I sighed. "What will you do?"

"We'll give him a proper funeral soon. Beyond that, I don't know."

We sat in silence for a few minutes.

"Don't let them win," she whispered.

"What do you mean?"

"They wanted to destroy you, didn't they?" I nodded. "Don't let them. We're going to need you, the girls and I. I know where you've been Gray, that place of despair. We pulled you out of it once. I don't know if I can do it again."

She was partly right. She didn't need me. Nancy was the strongest woman I knew. But looking into her eyes, I saw not a shred of blame, only love and compassion. We *were* family, that much I knew. And family didn't give up on each other.

"Okay," I said, and drifted into a peaceful, dreamless sleep.

29

I was out of the hospital by the end of the week, full of piss and vinegar. Frank's funeral was on Saturday, and I'd told the doctors in no uncertain terms that they'd have to kill me to keep me from going. Begrudgingly, they'd discharged me, still not knowing what to make of my recovery.

It was a somber affair, with lots of tears. Seeing the girls crying broke my heart, and I thought long and hard about drinking away the pain, but I'd promised Nancy I'd stay away from the bottle. Several people got up and said kind words about Frank and all he'd done for them, which only made saying goodbye that much harder. Part of me wanted to get up in front and say something too, but I didn't. The important people already knew how I felt.

After the funeral, I went home with Nancy and the girls to help fill the emptiness. There were plenty of things to do around the house, she'd told me, and the girls would appreciate the distraction.

When we pulled up in front, I noticed Frank's old Buick was parked in its usual spot. That got me thinking: how had those bastards gotten ahold of Frank in the first place? Then I remembered I'd never touched base with Brenda. I had no idea if Frank had gotten her to safety at the hotel. She could still be in trouble.

"Nancy," I said, then hesitated before finding the right words. "Where was Frank the night he was taken?"

"I don't know," she answered. "He called from the office that evening and said he had to run an errand, but he wouldn't say what it was."

"Did he take the car?"

"I assume so, but it was parked here when you called." Her breath caught. She waited until the girls got out, then whispered, "They were waiting for him, weren't they? When he got home."

I grunted. I didn't want to jump to any conclusions, but those were my thoughts as well. I'd check the car later.

I got out and quickly caught up to the girls.

"'Scuse me, ladies. I gotta pee," I lied.

Nancy unlocked the door, and I pushed my way past and did a quick sweep of the house as I made my way to the bathroom. I doubted anyone would try anything at this point—my gut told me the danger was past—but I had to make sure. It turned out we were safe for now.

Next, I called the hotel and asked if my room was still occupied. They said that it was, since I had never checked out, and that my credit card was being charged on a nightly basis. I assured them that that was as it should be and asked to be connected to the room. A few rings later, Brenda picked up.

"Hello," she said tentatively.

"Brenda, it's Gray. Are you all right?"

"Yes. I was wondering when you'd be in touch. I haven't heard anything since your partner dropped us off. What's going on?" Her words ran together, she was talking so fast.

I filled her in as best as I could, explaining that the data we got from her was being used as evidence and that she would likely be called in for questioning soon.

"I think you should be safe to go back home now," I told her. She sighed in relief. "Thank you. I really appreciate what you did. I don't know how I can repay you. This room alone has to be costing you a fortune."

"Yeah, probably," I laughed. "You can start by telling the police everything." I gave her Detective Rowe's number and said I'd be in touch.

***

On Monday, I went to the office and sat in silence for a

couple of hours. I wasn't sure what to do. I flipped through some case files but found it hard to get motivated. The phone rang once or twice, but I let it go to voice-mail.

I made coffee. I cleaned the kitchen. I stopped in Frank's doorway a few times but couldn't bring myself to go in. Not yet. I went for a walk. I called Mr. McCarthy to see how Ellie was doing. She was much better.

It was too quiet in the office. I missed Frank's annoying whistling. I found myself thinking about Brenda, wondering how she was doing in the aftermath of everything. Huh. There was a thought. She answered on the second ring.

"Hello?"

"Brenda, this is Gray. Do you need a job?" It turned out she did, so we made hasty arrangements for her to start working at the office the next day.

That settled, I laid down on the couch to take a nap. Just as I was drifting off, I heard *thunk, thunk*. Ha, it was kind of fitting. I pulled the phone out of my pocket: one new email. I opened it.

Mr. Gray, congratulations on your successful fishing trip. You landed a big one—it was quite entertaining to watch. But the waters you now travel are filled with even bigger ones. I advise against going out again. You would need a much bigger boat.

Entertaining to watch? So Harrison *had* been there. Hmm, that would explain the other four bodies. Interesting. I had a fuzzy recollection of Death hovering over me during the final struggle, carrying a scoped rifle. Maybe I wasn't that far off.

Even bigger fish in the water? I didn't like the sound of that.

I stretched back out on the couch. I would take his advice. I was done fishing. Time to hang up the rod.

I closed my eyes and went to sleep. I dreamt of very large boats.

Epilogue

Michael knocked on the heavy mahogany door. Even though he'd been summoned, manners were manners, and he would not enter without being personally invited.

"Enter," said Mr. Monday.

Michael pushed the door open and crossed the ancient Persian rug to stand behind his master, who was again surveying his domain.

"You have news?" Mr. Monday inquired.

"Yes. The rebels have disbanded. Elijah was killed, and the others have rejoined the fold."

"Good. Were there any complications?"

"None to speak of. The cattle were relocated successfully, and there are no connections outside of their limited business affairs." Michael paused, and his master sensed it.

"There is something else?"

"There were cameras in the ballroom."

"Have the footage erased."

"Yes, sir. But... I think you should watch it first."

Mr. Monday turned from the glass and regarded Michael curiously. It wasn't often someone gave him a suggestion. That could be... dangerous. He smiled, sending shivers down Michael's spine.

"Very well, then. Proceed."

Michael removed a small tablet from his jacket pocket and started the video. Mr. Monday watched without expression until Elijah was staggered by a punch. He arched an eyebrow. It remained that way until the video concluded.

"Most interesting," Mr. Monday remarked.

"Is he a threat?" asked Michael.

"Perhaps."

"Shall I have him removed?"

"Not yet. He may prove to be useful in the future." Mr. Monday turned back to the windows and returned a watchful eye to his realm.

Acknowledgements

Writing this book took a lot of time and I couldn't have done it without the help and support of some awesome people. I owe my beta readers a huge thanks who took something flawed and helped make it something I can be proud of. So... Erin Bradner, Christina Scott Sayer, and Sara Markham—**thank you**. I'd also like to thank my wife and four kids for putting up me; I'm sure it won't get any easier; and my mother, for being my cheerleader.

Most of all I'd like to thank my good friend and fellow author, Keith Potempa. He helped me take an idea, a character, and turn it into a story. If it weren't for him, I never would have finished this book.

About the Author

William lives in the beautiful Shenandoah Valley of Virginia with his wife and four children. He is an elementary school teacher and actor. He performs regularly in a Murder Mystery Dinner Theatre at a local resort and owns a traveling theatre company, Impressions Theatre, that performs in libraries during the summer. He holds a B.S. In Fisheries Science from Virginia Tech and an M.A. In Teaching from Mary Baldwin.

The idea for this novel came to him during a six-year period of time when he lived in Chicago pursuing a professional acting career.

For more information and updates on the next MASON GRAY CASE, visit his website at:
http://williamcmarkham.weebly.com